The Logic of Images

by the same author

Emotion Pictures

The Logic of Images

Essays and Conversations

Wim Wenders

Translated by Michael Hofmann

faber and faber

LONDON · BOSTON

First published in English in 1991
by Faber and Faber Limited
3 Queen Square London WC1N 3AU
First published in German in 1988
by Verlag der Autoren, Frankfurt, West Germany

Photoset by Parker Typesetting Service Leicester

Printed in Great Britain by Clays Ltd St Ives plc

A CIP record for this book is available from the British Library

ISBN 0-571-14208-7

CONTENTS

Why do you make films?
Reply to a questionnaire

Ever since this terrible question was put to me, I've done nothing but think of how to answer it. I have one answer in the morning and one at night, one at the editing-table, one when I'm looking at stills of earlier films of mine, another when I'm speaking to my accountant, and yet another when I think of the team I've been working with for years now. Every one of these different answers, these reasons for making films, is sincere and genuine, but I keep saying to myself there must be something 'more fundamental', some 'commitment', or even a 'compulsion'.

I was twelve years old when I made my very first film, with an 8 mm camera. I stood by a window and filmed the street below, the cars and pedestrians. My father saw me and asked: 'What are you doing with your camera?' And I said: 'Can't you see? I'm filming the street.' 'What for?' he asked. I had no answer. Ten or twelve years later, I was making my first short film in 16 mm. A reel of film lasted three minutes. I filmed a crossroads from the sixth floor, without moving the camera until the reel was finished. It didn't occur to me to pull away or stop shooting any earlier. With hindsight, I suppose it would have seemed like sacrilege to me.

Why sacrilege?

I'm no great theorist. I tend not to remember things I've read in books. So I can't give you Béla Balázs's exact words, but they affected me profoundly all the same. He talks about the ability (and the responsibility) of cinema 'to show things as they are'. And he says cinema can 'rescue the existence of things'.

That's precisely it.

I have another quote, from Cézanne, where he says: 'Things are disappearing. If you want to see anything, you have to hurry'.

So back to the awful question: why do I make films? Well, because . . . Something happens, you see it happening, you film it as it happens, the camera sees it and records it, and you can look at it again, afterwards. The thing itself may no longer be there, but you can still see it, the fact of its existence hasn't been lost. The act of filming is a heroic act (not always, not often, but sometimes). For a moment, the gradual destruction of the world of appearances is held up. The camera is a weapon against the tragedy of things, against their disappearing. Why make films? Bloody stupid question!

April 1987

Time Sequences, Continuity of Movement: *Summer in the City* and *The Goalkeeper's Fear of the Penalty*

Right at the beginning – and not much of that has survived – I thought making films meant setting the camera up somewhere, pointing it at some object, and then just letting it run. My favourite films were those made by the pioneer film-makers at the turn of the century, who purely recorded and were surprised by what they had captured. The mere fact that you could make an image of something in motion and replay it fascinated them. A train pulling into a station, a lady in a hat taking a step backwards, billowing steam and a stationary train. That's the kind of thing the early film-makers shot, cranking the camera by hand. They viewed it the next day, full of pride. What fascinated me about making films wasn't so much the possibility of altering or affecting or directing something, but simply watching it. Noticing or revealing things is actually much more precious to me than getting over some kind of message. There are films where you can't discover anything, where there's nothing to be discovered, because everything in them is completely unambiguous and obvious. Everything is presented exactly the way it's supposed to be understood. And then there are other films, where you're continually noticing little details, films that leave room for all kinds of possibilities. Those are mostly films where the images don't come complete with their interpretations.

Last year Robby Müller and I made a film called *Summer in the City*: it's shot in 16 mm black and white, it's two and a half hours long, and we shot it in six days. It had a screenplay, more or less, so that when we see the film now we're pretty sure what parts of it we were responsible for – mostly the framing and the dialogue – and what was left to chance. The way the film turned out, there's something almost private about it, the people who appeared in it were friends, it was all shot straight off, we only went for a second take when something went totally wrong. That first film could have been of any length: it was my graduation film at film-school. It started off at three hours, but that seemed too long to me, so now it's two and a half. There's a shot in it of a cinema in Berlin and it's held for two minutes without anything happening, just because I happened to like the cinema; it was called the Urania. Or we drove the length of the Kudamm, shooting out of the car window. In the film that lasts eight minutes, just as long it took to shoot. We wouldn't have been able to use that shot of the cinema in *The Goalkeeper*: it would have been impossible, a withdrawal into an attitude of pure contemplation. It would have left a hole that the rest of the film would have disappeared into. The eight-minute drive would have had to be intercut with something else, and even then it couldn't have gone on for eight minutes. In *Summer in the City* we drove through a tunnel in Munich, and I filmed out of the side window of the car. We drove through this long tunnel and out the other side. For about a minute all you see on the screen is blackness, with the occasional headlight, and when I did the mixing, the man who sits at the back and puts on the tapes came up and said to me that there were a lot of things he liked about the film, but why on earth didn't I cut when we drove into the tunnel. And when I said: 'The tunnel was half a mile long, and we couldn't do it any quicker,' he gave me a look and said: 'You can't do that'. I should take a look at his films sometime; he made 8 mm films, he'd been to Romania and he'd made this twenty-minute film that showed you everything there was to see in Romania. And he got very angry, though he'd been friendly to begin with. Yet it seemed to me that we'd done a lot of things earlier in the film that might easily have provoked him much more, but none of it made him as angry as the fact that I hadn't switched off the camera when we'd entered the tunnel. When people think they've seen enough of something, but there's more, and no change of shot, then they react in a curiously livid way. They think there must be some justification for it, but it never occurs to them that the fact that you happen to like whatever is in the shot is sufficient justification. They imagine there has to be some other reason, and when they can't find it they get mad. It makes them madder than when a film actually insults them – which can happen too.

I think it's really important for films to be sequential. Anything that disturbs or breaks up these sequences annoys me. Films have got to respect these sequences of action – even highly stylized films, like the one we're making at the moment, *The Goalkeeper's Fear of the Penalty*. The continuity of movement and action must be true, there mustn't be any jolt in the time being portrayed. You see a lot of cuts like that now, especially in TV films, where they cut back and forth: close-up of some-one speaking, cut to close-up of someone else listening, then back to the first person again – and you can just tell from his face that time has elapsed, time that you haven't been shown, because the whole thing's been 'tightened up'. I hate that, and it makes me angry whenever I see it happening. Doesn't matter what kind of film it is, I just think it should keep faith with the passage of time – even when it's not a 'realistic' film at all, but something quite artificial. There more than anywhere you have to observe certain rules, particularly visual rules. I hate abstract films where each image is somehow a separate thought, and where the sum of the images and thoughts is something quite arbitrary. Films are congruent time-sequences, not congruent ideas. Even a change of location is some-thing I have difficulty with. In every scene, my biggest problem is always how to end it and go on to the next one. Ideally, I would show the time in between as well. But sometimes you just have to leave it out, it simply takes too long; so when someone leaves his house and turns up some-where else, you leave out all the intervening time. Someone leaves the pub and goes back to his room, and for me it's terrible not to be able to show him going up the stairs. On the film I'm working on right now, it's the hardest thing. How do you cut this: he goes to bed at night, and then it's the following morning and he's having breakfast. Every time, I have to think: how do they manage that in films, how do they get from one day to the next? It's a problem even at the screenplay stage, cutting off an action that you know is actually continuing. In the end, the film just cuts somewhere. Every action – everything the goalkeeper does in our film, for instance – everything continues, and what you show is actually just a part of it. That's the hardest thing for me, how to choose what to show.

I spoke to a journalist the other day, someone who practically knew the novel by heart, and he quizzed me about specific passages in it, about how I'd managed to film them, and I got really scared. And yet all that's over and done with, really, how close the film is to the book, or if it's got anything to do with the book at all. Now someone's seen a print, and he said a particular scene seemed to him just exactly the way he remembered it in the book. And I couldn't even say whether it was in the book at all, or how it had been there, and I was just astounded that someone should come to me and say it was just like in the book. Actually, what interested me in the book wasn't so much the 'Handke' part of it as the writing: the way things were described, the way it moved from one sentence to the next. You suddenly felt completely hooked, because each sentence was so good on its own, the sequence of sentences suddenly seemed much more engrossing than the action and the question what, if anything, will happen next. I loved that about the book. How each sentence flows from the one before. That precision is what gave me the idea of making a film, and of making it in a similar way too, using images in sequence like Handke uses his sentences, images with the same truthfulness and precision. That's what made the film so expensive to make, because achieving that sort of precision takes a great deal of trouble, making our images reminiscent of certain types of shot that you see a lot in American films, for instance, or using a particular kind of light that is difficult to produce. Because the images will 'click' only when you have that exact quality of light, which is quite tricky to create.

I feel this is all a bit imprecise, but somehow, ever since making the film, I've stopped thinking about it on a theoretical level. I always wanted to make something simple, nothing too specialized and sophisticated. Not in order to be ingratiating, but maybe to hold the interest of people who'll only go to see it because they like football. I've avoided doing things that would simply antagonize people. The film seems straightforward enough to me. There's nothing mysterious or obscure or enigmatic about it, although that actually seems to be the hardest thing of all to grasp: that really there isn't anything more to it than what you see on the screen in front of you, and that Bloch is what Bloch does and no more. Perhaps because I've tried to keep the film simple a lot of people will find it incomprehensible, because they'll feel obliged to look for more than they're actually seeing.

September 1971

The Scarlet Letter

'I wish my life was a non-stop Hollywood movie show 'cause celluloid
heroes never feel any pain . . .'

The Kinks

A friend asked me what was I doing, making a film where I couldn't have
cars or garages or slot-machines. I replied: 'Just because . . .' – but I
wasn't really convinced. That was before we started filming *The Scarlet
Letter*. Now apart from the screenplay, the sets and the actors, what
reality can you put into a film that's based on a nineteenth-century novel
with a seventeenth-century plot?

We started filming in an underground studio in Cologne. We would
finish late in the afternoon and ride up to daylight in the lift. It was like
coming out of a mine. I was amazed it was still light, and every day I
thought of getting a camera up out of the studio and filming the actors as
they emerged, dazzled and blinking. I thought I owed it to the light.

On our last day in Cologne, Yella – who plays the little girl in the film
– was in tears, because the sets were being taken down.

We started the location filming by the sea on the north west coast of
Spain. On one occasion we were prevented from filming by the presence
of a tanker on the horizon. Our own ship was a three-master. It was
made of cardboard and it hung in the air, suspended from wires, just ten
yards away from the camera. Once when Hans Christian Blech was
filming the sea with his own 8 mm camera during a break in the shooting,
I felt a wild urge to put him in the film, in costume, eagerly filming the
Puritans. In *The Scarlet Letter* he never gets near any technical
equipment.

In the Western-style village outside Madrid where we were shooting
for the last fortnight, there was a two-storey saloon which – unlike the
rest of the houses – we weren't allowed to tinker with, to make it fit into

a seventeenth-century New England town. So it wasn't ever allowed to come into shot. We would eat lunch in that saloon, sitting at long tables, but such genuine and arresting images of ourselves in the saloon (which we never shot) weren't allowed to appear in a film from which reality had to be strictly excluded, cut away like the bad bit of an apple. The single exception was a seagull that once flew through a shot.

Every film is also a documentary of itself and the way it was made. For me, *The Scarlet Letter* documents conditions under which I wouldn't care to work again: I don't ever want to make another film in which a car or a petrol station or a television set or a phone booth aren't allowed to appear.

That sounds emotive, but emotion is what it's about: emotion is only possible in films which haven't been subjected to restrictive conditions, and which don't subject the things in them to such conditions either, whether it's the actors, or the sky overhead, or a dog trotting past in the back of the shot. That said, the children in *The Scarlet Letter* contradict everything I've written here. They're as natural as they are in a science-fiction film.

March 1973

The heroes are the others

An interview with Peter Handke and Wim Wenders on *False Movement*

What is the relationship between Goethe's Wilhelm Meister *and your screenplay for* False Movement?

HANDKE: I've long wanted to do a *Wilhelm Meister*. In Goethe's book Wilhelm Meister travels across Germany in a single sweeping movement. Something similar happened to me the first time I went to Germany and travelled about for a couple of months; I felt this absolute movement through a country, and of course the pathos of someone embarking on a new life. That spurred me on; also I wanted to show someone with ideals, someone who lived by them, even if they were just coyly expressed dreams, and wanted to become something, I mean an artist.

It wasn't unusual for me, just using one or two things from Goethe that had lodged in my memory. They – together with the idea of movement – fed the whole script. I wasn't aiming at a total reconstruction of the story; I was just taking the historical situation of someone setting out, going on the road, trying to learn something, become somebody different, just become somebody. I'm pretty sure that that's what Goethe had in mind too: a movement, or the attempt at a movement. Where the difference lies is in consciousness and in the German landscape, which have both changed a great deal and have turned rather miserable. What Goethe had a couple of hundred years ago as a great gesture, a great movement, a great journey, being on the road, setting off, in my version is possible only in little moments of rebellion that fizzle out, are extinguished by what has changed in the landscape, and, of course, also in the inner life of the guy who calls himself the hero. The heroic allure of Wilhelm Meister is beyond him, even if he tries to see himself as the hero of his personal story. He keeps setting off on really serious, monumental movements. But who can live like that, where every possibility can be computed? But he wants to attain it. And so it starts in this epic way: the sea, love, a love scene; you see someone standing on a platform, then on a train, and you go towards them, and you think, now, there's eternity in this, and it'll come off – but not in the story the way I've written it. It does in Goethe, but not with me. And then the narrow streets of a town that might still look the way it did in Goethe's time, with half-timbered houses – but you can't get into it properly. In Goethe, you get walks in the town; he describes them. That's not on any more, because of the traffic and the industrial landscape outside the town. So much for the external part.

And then there's his own story, where he comes from and his reasons for setting out. The story is full of moments of bewilderment, plaintiveness and discouragement, which are the consequence of his previous enthusiasm. That's the thing that really interests me about the book, that great movement that keeps appearing in the form of rage or an outburst of authentic feeling, but that keeps stumbling and collapsing into the quotidian – not exactly pathos, but into a humdrum realism – when your rage and your desire to lead the life you dream of can suddenly no longer be squared with the piddling constellations of reality, and you can't find the exaltation to lift off for the duration of a whole story. It was in that weird toing and froing that I found the kind of tension that this story can have for us today.

There's another great difference between Goethe's Meister *and* False Movement. *Goethe supplies the reader with a very precise depiction of the historical background of late feudalism and the rise of the middle classes. In your version, contemporary society is only evident in little signs, in ciphers.* HANDKE: That's right. But I don't think Goethe ever intended a precise depiction of society; I think he saw all these things as theatrical hooks, the Moravian Brethren or whatever, debt collection, you should see all that as a kind of romantic agitation, as dramatic business. It's not a real portrait of the times. He has ramifying theatrical plots, I have symbols.

What fascinated me much more was the desire to exist outside conditions created by others, and the subsequent failure to achieve that – the tension between those two states interested me.

What sort of character is Wilhelm in your screenplay? He seems so cool and remote, even though he's the hero. HANDKE: I see him as indefinable. He's got a kind of hunger, he's eager to learn. Women are attracted to him. And then I thought that might have something sexually attractive about it – someone who sets off in pursuit of something. It's so boyish. There's something wistful about him. He has these impulses, but actually he's only ever impressive when he's with other people, listening to them. So I wanted him to spend a lot of time in company, not saying much. If you see him listening a lot, it makes him less plaintive.

Wilhelm Meister isn't really the hero at all. The heroes in the story are the individuals like the industrialist in his house, or the actress. Wilhelm attracts them to him, but only in order to get them to reveal something of themselves. They have far more courage and intensity than he does. He's just curious, and rather invulnerable. He keeps saying he wants to write. One day he'll put down what he's seen. The heroes are the others.

WENDERS: I'm not sure if it actually works out that way, because anyone who appears in a lot of scenes, and who – unlike the others – keeps on appearing, automatically becomes the main character in the film, or if you like, its hero. Everything is seen through his eyes, is introduced into the film via him. For instance, the actress is brought in through him.

But in spite of that, there's really very little about Wilhelm that's heroic; he seems so awkward and repressed. You see him sitting there, pretending not to be interested in what's going on. But then, he's driven by his indefinable compulsion to write; he'll try to set down those very things he's claimed to have ignored. It's the others who are active, he isn't.

HANDKE: Yes, he has something of the narrator. You can imagine that he might have written the screenplay himself, because he's so objective about himself. He's completely without self-love – the way you love some things you describe in order to be identified with them. It's the opposite with him. What identification he does feel at the beginning, where he's often alone by the sea or whatever, he tries to break up by seeking out the company of other people. So you really can imagine that he's written it all. There are films like that, with a first-person narrator.

WENDERS: I think I made it very clear in the first two shots of the film that he's the person the story's about, but at the same time the things you get to see are a part of him too. The first shot is flying across the River

Elbe, until you see the town of Glückstadt. Then it moves lower until you see the whole of the marketplace and the church. Then there's a cut, and in the next shot you see the marketplace and the church out of a window, and there's a helicopter passing behind the church, and then the camera withdraws and shows you who's just seen the helicopter, which is Wilhelm looking out of the window. So the film begins with a narrative position like Goethe's, from above and all-seeing. And then it goes into a subjective view. I think those first two shots make the blend clear: that it's someone's story that is being told, and also that he's dramatizing himself.

May 1975

Kings of the Road*

This film is the story of two men, but it doesn't take a Hollywood approach to the subject. American films about men – especially recent ones – are exercises in suppression: the men's true relationships with women, or with each other, are displaced by story, action and the need to entertain. They leave out the real nub: why the men prefer to be together, why they get on with each other, why they don't get on with women, or, if they do, then only as a pastime. My film is about precisely that: two men getting on together, each preferring the other's company to that of a woman. You get to see the shortcomings of both of them, their emotional insecurity; you see them trying to be mutually supportive and to hide their faults. But with the passage of time they're no longer bothered by these faults, and when they know each other well enough they begin discussing them. As a consequence of that, they split up. They split up because, on their journey across Germany, they've suddenly grown too close. It's a story that you're not often told in films about men. The story of the absence of women, which is at the same time the story of the longing for their presence!

Doing the recce for *False Movement*, I kept coming across locations I couldn't use because that story didn't call for them. In the end I saw so many places that I liked in Germany that I wished I didn't have a fixed story to follow. So I decided to make my next project a travelling film where I could put in anything I liked, where I would have the freedom of making up the story as we – literally – went along. A film that, even when we were halfway through shooting it, could still change totally.

The idea of the truck came to me somewhere on the Autobahn I think between Frankfurt and Würzburg, when I had to drive along for miles behind two trucks which kept overtaking each other. I felt pretty angry

*The literal translation of the German title, *Im Lauf der Zeit*, is *In the Course of Time*.

with them, but when I finally managed to pass them I got a glimpse of the guys inside. It was a hot day and one of them was dangling his leg out of the window, and they were talking. It struck me that it must be quite pleasant, rolling along in a juggernaut, slowly and steadily; sleeping in it at night. I stopped at a lorry-drivers' caff, and I liked the atmosphere there a lot, the way they were with each other, their politeness and attentiveness. There was this snug and secure feeling. I thought I might make my film about lorry drivers driving across Germany. To begin with, I thought of a travelling circus or a fair. But that would have entailed long stopovers in each place, and I wanted the film to get a move on. Later I had the idea of somehow using village cinemas in the film, and then suddenly it all clicked. It even gave me the fixed points for my itinerary: cinemas.

From the distributors I got a large wall-map of Germany marking all the places with cinemas, and I drew up a route with over eighty cinemas on it, just along the border with East Germany, between Lüneburg and Passau. I chose that route because it's a long way off the main north–south routes in Germany. I took a fortnight and looked at all the cinemas. Many that were still listed on the distributors' map were already gone. I took photos of cinemas like a maniac and barely looked at anything else. When I got back, I made a selection of twelve cinemas, almost all of which appear in the final film. Then I went on a second trip with Mike and Robby, my executive producer and cameraman. We looked at the twelve cinemas again and saw what else there was to see, in those places and on the road. Finally, just before we were about to start filming, I went off on a third trip concentrating on the landscapes and the people. But I abandoned that, because there was just too much. And then we started shooting. We had a storyline for the first few days, no more. Thereafter, there was just our route with its fixed points: a few village cinemas in Lower Saxony, Hessen and Bavaria.

There was no screenplay, which was just what I wanted. But when we were about to start shooting I suffered nights of anxiety – should I structure the thing a bit more? And then a couple of times, in a panic, I started writing some feeble conclusion. Even after we started shooting I was still afraid that everything would go wrong. Then, in Wolfsburg, we got the bad news that the whole of the first week's filming was unusable on account of a fault in the stock, and we'd have to reshoot it all. At first that floored me, but when I'd taken it in, it was suddenly liberating: what else can possibly go wrong now? Now we can go flat out! Our shooting schedule was completely useless anyway because of the mishap of the first week. Now we were ready for anything. We decided that a group of five of us would write the story: the two actors, the cameraman, my assistant and me. And for a while we managed to keep that up, but it meant it was two or three in the morning before we had the next day's scenes ready. It exhausted us. We didn't get much sleep, but the really shattering thing was trying to weld five imaginations into one. That really took it out of us. We meant to carry on, though, and it was only our growing tiredness that forced us to change tack. So from about the third week of shooting I did the writing in the evening with Martin, who typed, and then we went over the new scenes in the morning with the others. We kept that up until the seventh week, admittedly with lengthening pauses to recuperate. Finally we all felt completely physically wrecked. We had a two-week break in the filming. We'd covered just half the route. The end was miles off, and it looked more uncertain than ever.

At night, in some village hotel room, I would sometimes be overcome with terror. I would be sitting around, and it would be midnight, or two or four in the morning, and I still had no idea what we'd be shooting in the morning . . . and with fifteen people on the payroll! Once or twice the next day would arrive and I still wouldn't have any idea. Then we'd all sit around on location for a couple of gloomy hours and then push off back to the hotel. I think I needed those occasions just to realize what we were about. For the first time, I made the connection between money and ideas in making a film. Normally when you're filming you aren't aware that ideas carry price tags. In this film, though, there was often a direct link: if I haven't managed to finish this page by tomorrow, I'll be 3000 marks out of pocket. And then I would say to myself, all right, stuff the 3000 marks, I'm tired, and I need time to think.

It only occurred to me to make this film because I knew I had the right team for it. The very notion of making a film with that degree of freedom depended from the start on my wanting to work with people whom I'd already worked with under different circumstances, in such a way that they could now all contribute as much as possible. I knew they too wanted to make a film in that way, and I think that, though it sometimes got tough, everyone enjoyed it.

I wanted a completely cinematic feel. Working with Robby guaranteed that. He knew that the language of the film would be cinematic, but that it would be made under entirely new circumstances. We wanted our adventure to show in the film, but not in its style or its appearance. We did a lot of practice shoots beforehand, with the actors and the truck. Hansi Dreher devised and built a camera harness for the truck, we tried out various film stock and filters. And we used the new Zeiss lenses, which are phenomenally sharp. We were going for depth, sharpness of focus and high contrast. That was the visual style, and for that we needed an awful lot of light. Even when we were filming out of doors we used screens or lights wherever possible. The last thing I wanted was for it to look like a documentary film. That's also why we put the camera on tracks a lot and used crane shots.

I knew from the start that the film would be in black and white. Whenever I thought of the story, it was always in black and white. A lot of that was to do with the truck, which would just have looked exotic in colour. It was orange! Ever since *Alice in the Cities* Robby and I had wanted to work in black and white again. It's a pity that black and white has become the exception. It would be good for quite a lot of films if they'd been shot in black and white. For me, black and white is more realistic than colour. Black and white can be colourful, and colour can be very black and white.

I learned a lot about the condition of rural cinemas, especially from the recces. It was noticeable that most of these cinemas belonged to women, especially older women, who went on running them with a real passion, and against any economic sense. They were well aware of the fact that there was no one to take over from them and that their cinemas would perish with them. Maybe that was why they were so determined. There were women who worked hard all day running a pub, just in order to hold on to their cinema. It made no money, they even had to subsidize it. 'Oh, but it wouldn't be a life without the cinema.' The distributors – those who still bothered to supply these village cinemas – treated these women like dirt. For instance, none of these cinemas was allowed to determine its own programme, or ask for anything: if they wanted to be supplied, they had to take a whole package, all that demeaning crap that only runs in sleazy downtown areas in cities. As a result, people who go to the cinema in the country are so unused to ever getting anything worth seeing that they've come to accept that garbage as 'cinema', and that's how the distributors justify themselves in continuing to distribute it. In their rural operation, the distributors now work only with guarantee contracts, say 80 or 100 marks per film. If the box office doesn't bring in that much, the cinema-owners have to make up the difference from their own pockets. I doubt if there's another business in Germany that's as badly exploited and exploitative as that. It's glaringly obvious that a couple of years from now there will not be a single person left who will put up with this situation and that'll be the end of the rural cinema. *Kings of the Road* is also a film about the end of the cinema.

But for rock music, I'd have gone crazy. The Velvet Underground have got this line: 'Her life was saved by rock and roll'. That's why Bruno keeps a jukebox in the back of his truck, and a Dansette in the cab: two pieces of lifesaving equipment. In a way, the film is about the generation of men who spent their first pocket money on 'Tutti Frutti' or 'I'm Just a Lonely Boy', but who weren't old enough to wear pointed shoes. Standing wistfully around the scooters, watching some bloke riding around with his girl, pushing his hand up her shirt. They're thirty now, '2000 light years from home' just as they always were. It's all gotta change.

1976

The American Friend

I've wanted to film a book by Patricia Highsmith ever since I first read one, almost ten years ago. Each new novel of hers was an event for me. At the beginning of *The Goalkeeper's Fear of the Penalty* Josef Bloch goes into a cinema where he sees the cashier whom he kills later on. The title in big letters on the cinema billboard is: *The Tremor of Forgery*. Actually it wasn't a film at all, but the title of the Highsmith book I was reading during the filming in Vienna. Her stories have a kind of fascination for me that I usually only find in films. The characters in them affect me directly and powerfully. It is the characters that produce Highsmith's stories, not the other way round. Usually in crime fiction characters are shaped by plot and action; they are products not producers. Her stories spring from the fears, the petty cowardice and tiny acts of misconduct so familiar to everyone that you hardly observe them in yourself. As you read her novels, you learn about yourself. An innocuous little lie, a convenient self-deception gradually swells into a sinister tale, whose pull you can't escape because you understand it so well. It could just as easily happen to you. That's why these stories are so truthful; that's why, for all their fictitiousness, their subject is actually the truth. They reveal the extraordinary menace of the little cop-out, the mediocre inclination to be easy on yourself or on someone else. Nor are these stories psychologizing. On the contrary, they never explain. Their psychology is empirical. They aren't there to illustrate theories. Everything in them is particular. Everyone is individual; there are no examples and no generalizations.

That's why her stories are close to my work, which to me is more about documenting than manipulating. I want my films to be about the time in which they are filmed, and to reflect the cities, landscapes, objects and people involved in them, myself included. *Ripley's Game* left me that freedom. Because it's already there in the way Highsmith works. That's why I believe I've remained faithful to the book, whatever liberties I've taken with it. There is no such thing as the 'film version'. There are two separate things: books and films. They may share the same 'attitude' to things, but not possibly the same things.

Jonathan's life is turned upside down. He himself is turned upside down. Is he the man he always thought he was, or is there someone else inside him? What is he capable of? Is he defined by his life, his family, his job? Who is he, in the face of death? Is he anyone at all? And Tom Ripley, commuting between Europe and America, the way other people commute between work and home? What does that do to him? 'I'm less and less sure of who I am, or who anyone else is,' he mumbles into his tape recorder.

No other medium can treat the question of identity as searchingly or with as much justification as film. No other language is as capable of addressing itself to the physical reality of things. 'The possibility and the purpose of film is to show everything the way it is.' However exalted that sentence of Béla Balász sounds, it's true. Reading it makes me want to see a film. Or think up one myself. Load a camera and shoot something. The question of identity is new because it's no longer self-evident. I often think it's something women have a better grasp of than men. Children too, before they get it knocked out of them. The cinema will shine a light on it.

Every film is political. Most political of all are those that pretend not to be: 'entertainment' movies. They are the most political films there are because they dismiss the possibility of change. In every frame they tell you everything's fine the way it is. They are a continual advertisement for things as they are. I think *The American Friend* is different. Yes, it's 'entertainment' and it's exciting. But it doesn't affirm the status quo. On the contrary: everything is fluid, open, under threat. The film has no explicit political content. But it doesn't talk down to you. It doesn't treat its characters like marionettes – nor its audience either. A lot of 'political' films, unfortunately, do.

After my last film, *Kings of the Road*, which was made without a 'story' and almost without a script, I felt like working within the solid framework of a story provided by someone else. However, despite my faith in Patricia Highsmith's stories, it still wasn't easy for me to move freely within the one I chose: everything in the story seemed to be striving to get away from it. The characters all seemed to want to go in a different direction from the one Highsmith had prescribed for them. Jonathan seemed to want to become less hesitant, Marianne less detached but more confident, Ripley less unscrupulous, more sensitive. So it came about once more that I found myself staying up half the night, working on the script, right through the filming. If you penetrate so deeply into someone else's story, you notice its weaknesses. But you feel its strengths too. On many occasions the solution to a scene's problems was none other than what Highsmith had written in *Ripley's Game*. I'd merely forgotten it.

On the other hand, I found some other aspects of the book harder and harder to reconcile myself to, for instance the background story with the Mafia and the character of Minot. Why does he get involved in the story, what does he want? A lot of that ended up on the cutting-room floor. From the very first time I read the book, something bothered me about the Mafia turning up in it. I tried to make their presence more comprehensible to me by changing their business from gambling casinos to making porn films. At least I could imagine that, and I knew a bit about film producers and distributors. That's also the reason why I cast film directors as the gangsters, because they're the only rascals I know, and the only ones who make life and death decisions as airily as the Mafia. Even so, it remained a problem. I think maybe Patricia Highsmith found it one herself, otherwise she wouldn't have had such a bloodbath at the end: having summoned them in the first place, she had to get rid of them.

1977

Reverse angle: New York City, March 1982

'It was night, it was another arrival at another airport, in another city. For the first time in his life, he felt he'd had enough of travelling. All cities were as one to him. Something reminded him of a book he must have read in his childhood. His only dim memory of it was this feeling of being lost somewhere, which he felt again today . . .'

A story or a film might begin with those words, or words like that. Cut to a close-up of the hero. But this film can't start like that. This film has no story. What's it about, then?

I don't like talking about myself. Yes, I make films, and most of my films are very personal. But they're never private.

When I was asked a couple of weeks ago whether I'd like to make a kind of film-diary, a 'Letter from New York' for a film programme on French television, I was tempted by the opportunity to pick up a camera myself for the first time in ages and film something without any story, just 'to make pictures'. One might think that, as someone who has made ten movies, I would see my calling as telling stories in pictures. But that never quite convinced me. Maybe because basically pictures have always meant more to me than stories, yes, and sometimes the stories were merely a hook for hanging pictures.

But you can't always rely on pictures; they're not always there when you want them. On the contrary, they sometimes seem to avoid me, sometimes for weeks on end, even months. In all that time, I won't see a thing that strikes me, that seems 'worth preserving'. I completely lose any inclination to make pictures myself, and if I try my hand at it anyway, the results are completely random, images without form: because the eye that might have given them form isn't there. And then you can end up with the worst view there is: that of the tourist. The uncommitted view, the Evil Eye.

Right now too, without the brace of a story, images are starting to look interchangeable and purposeless to me, and things, searching for their lost form, look up through the camera lens at me and say: 'Why are you bothering us? Leave us in peace!' For me that spells the beginning of a new age hostile to images (and an age of hostile images too), and I run around with my camera in circles of despair. There's no help from the cinema; on the contrary, new American films are looking more and more like trailers for themselves. So much in America tends to self-advertisement, and that leads to an invasion of and inflation of meaningless images. And television, as ever, at the forefront. Optical toxin.

After days of this blindness, it's two books that once more open my eyes to pictures and put me in the mood for peaceful looking: a novel by Emmanuel Bove, who observes and relates his subjects simply and with great respect for detail, and a book of reproductions of Edward Hopper's paintings. These books remind me that the camera is capable of equally careful description, and that things can appear through it in a good light: the way they are.

With these newly acquired images, a new story can begin right away: 'She sat by the window, waiting. She looked up at the cloudless sky, and then down over the expanse of park, and let time pass . . .'

At the same time as this film, another bit of 'picture-making' is nearing its conclusion: I'm editing *Hammett*, my first Hollywood-made American film. Three editors are working on it, in three suites on three cutting-tables at once. This impersonal way of working is totally unlike my own experience of cutting. I get the feeling neither the story nor the pictures belong to me. They are the property of the studio and the producer.

One night I appear on a talk show with Tony Richardson. Louis Malle was announced as well, but apparently he's unable to come. We talk, inevitably, about the difference between European and American cinema. It's less than electrifying.

A more precise examination of that difference is the film I made last year, during an eight-month break in the shooting of *Hammett*. This film is called *The State of Things*, and it ends in a caravan going up and down Hollywood Boulevard all night long. 'The producer' and 'the director' have a long talk which ends with this song, shortly before both of them die:

Hollywood, Hollywood,
never been a place people had it so good
like Hollywood, like Hollywood.

What do you do with your life, my friend,
in Hollywood, in Hollywood.

The producer of *Hammett*, Francis Ford Coppola, is coming to New York for the last few days of editing. We arrange several showings in a preview theatre on Broadway in front of sample audiences we bring in off the street. Afterwards, the two of us discuss at length the last few cuts and changes.

In front of the house where I'm staying in New York, you can see a bit of the granite rock the city's been built on. I hope my next film, the next story, will be about this rock. During work on the script, I come across this quote from the painter Paul Cézanne: 'Things are looking bad. You have to hurry if you want to see anything. Everything is disappearing.'
    I hope it's not too late.

March 1982

Chambre 666

By the side of the motorway, close to the turn-off to the Paris airport of Roissy, stands a majestic tree which for years now has waved me good-bye when I've left Europe and welcomed me back when I've returned. My old friend is a Lebanese cedar at least 150 years old. The last time I drove past it, I was on my way to the festival at Cannes. The tree had a message for me. It reminded me that it had been around when photography was just beginning, that it had lived through all of film history to the present day, and that in all probability it would still be there when there were no more films.

So when I arrived in Cannes, I had a question for my colleagues. In room 666 at the Hotel Martinez a 16 mm camera was set up, a microphone and a Nagra, also a television set with the sound off. There was a chair and a table with a sheet of paper with my question on it. The directors (whoever was contactable in Cannes; many, of course, due to pressure of work or lack of time or for whatever reason, didn't appear) were informed about my project; they were able to consider their replies at leisure, switch on the camera and tape recorder for themselves, and turn them off again when they had finished.

The text of my question read:
Increasingly, films are looking as though they had been made for television, as regards their lighting, framing and rhythm. It looks as though a television aesthetic has supplanted film aesthetic.

Many new films no longer refer to any reality outside the cinema – only to experiences contained in other films – as though 'life' itself no longer furnished material for stories.

Fewer films get made. The trend is towards increasingly expensive super-productions at the expense of the 'little' film.

And a lot of films are immediately available on video cassettes. That market is expanding rapidly. Many people prefer to watch films at home.

So my question is:

Is cinema becoming a dead language, an art which is already in the process of decline?

JEAN-LUC GODARD:

How long is the reel? Fine.

I've got this piece of paper that Wim Wenders gave me. He's set up a camera and a tape recorder and left me here. But he hasn't set me up properly; I can still see them playing tennis on the television. I'll play ball – I'll play the fool.

This is an enquiry about the future of the cinema. It appears, it says on the paper, that a television aesthetic has replaced a cinematic aesthetic for large parts of the audience all over the world.

Well, you have to know who invented television and what the context was. Its arrival coincided with the talkies, at a time when governments were half-consciously thinking of harnessing the incredible power that was released by the silent film, which, unlike painting, achieved instant popularity.

Rembrandt's paintings and Mozart's music were supported by kings and princes. But it was a mass public that very quickly came to support the cinema. The silent movie was something to behold: first you look, then you speak. The sound film might have been invented right away, but that didn't happen. Instead, it took thirty years.

The age of reason. Whoever has power has right on his side, you might say. First came the technical birth of television. When the film people weren't interested in it, it had to be rescued by the post office, people working in communications. So today, television is like a little post office. It's nothing to be afraid of, it's so small and you have to be very close to the picture. In the cinema, on the other hand, the picture is large and intimidating, and you watch it from some way away. Today, it seems people would rather look at a small picture close up than a large one from a distance.

Television emerged very quickly because it was born in the USA. It was born at the very same time as the advertising that financed it. So it was the highly articulate advertising world, saying things in a single phrase or image, like Eisenstein, as good as Eisenstein, as good as *Potemkin*. So they made ads like *Potemkin*, only *Potemkin* is ninety minutes long.

Is cinema dying out as a language, will it soon be a defunct art form?

It really doesn't matter. It's bound to happen some time. I shall die, but will my art die? I remember telling Henri Langlois that he should throw away his collection of films and go off somewhere, otherwise he would die. So one should just go off somewhere. It's much the better way.

Films are created when there's no one looking. They are the Invisible. What you can't see is the Incredible – and it's the task of the cinema to show you that.

I'm sitting here in front of the camera, but in reality, in my head, I'm behind it. My world is the imaginary, and that's a journey between forwards and backwards, between to and fro. Like Wim, I'm a great traveller.

OK. See you later.

PAUL MORRISSEY:
'Cinema is a language that's on the way out, an art that will soon be dead.'

Yes, I agree. Clearly, it's getting near the end. No grounds for thinking anything else. The novel, as everyone knows, is already long dead. Poetry's been exhausted for a hundred years. There aren't any more plays – just the odd one now and then. And a film every so often too. But that's just about it.

The cinema is being supplanted by TV, yes, right. For myself, I prefer television to most films. I think the cinema's dying for the same reason as the novel did earlier. The novel was alive as long as it depended on characters, as long as it gave the writer the opportunity to invent characters. People used to read such novels. And they went to the theatre to see plays by Shakespeare, Shaw, Molière, whoever – because they had good characters. The content of these plays, their message, philosophy, politics, all that's beside the point, it doesn't matter. Most of it's ridiculous and stupid, and dates very quickly. But good characters, they last.

Now you don't get them in the cinema any more. The things that count in the cinema today are godawful things like directing and cinematography.

I prefer television, because it's where you still get human beings. In television there's no directorial ambition – that's why there's more life in television than in the cinema. That's where you see characters, in the sitcoms and the soaps, whether they're family sagas or adventures. Maybe television will die some day too, I don't know.

MIKE DE LEONE:
It's nonsense asking a Filipino director like myself about the future of the cinema. The future of the Filipino cinema is inseparable from the question of the future of the Philippines.

MONTE HELLMAN:
I don't go to the cinema much nowadays. I have a video recorder, and I tape films off the television. I don't watch them while I'm recording them, and only rarely do I watch them later. I've got a collection of about 200 films that I never look at.

I really think it makes no odds if the cinema's getting to be more like TV or vice versa, or if the language of film is changing. I don't think film is dying. There are good times and bad times. The last few years were bad: there weren't a lot of films that I wanted to go and see, and what I did see was usually disappointing. When I see a film that annoys me, then I usually go and look out an old movie that I know and like. And I usually get some stimulus from that.

ROMAIN GOUPIL:
If you look at the development of television, and its incredible ability to beam out films all over the world by satellite, or that amazing device video, well, then I do feel that cinema as we know it is on the way out.

Even while I was making my film *Mourir à Trente Ans* I would sometimes have this feeling that it was all out of date. Magnetic sound-recording, all the lab processing, the things you have to do to a film – how cumbersome and time-consuming it all is, when all you're doing is trying to tell a story.

SUSAN SEIDELMAN:
Let me just say this for myself. I think films are about passion. You make a film in the same way as you paint a picture: you have an intense feeling

for something, you love life, and you want to communicate that. And you express it in a certain form. When the passion goes out of cinema, then it'll start to die, just like any other art form.

NOËL SIMSOLO:
No, it's not the cinema that's dead, it's the film-makers who make moronic films. People die because they're not allowed to make the films they want to. But that's another story . . .

RAINER WERNER FASSBINDER:
This diagnosis of a cinema that resembles television more and more is really no longer relevant. It may have been the case between 1974 and 1977, say, but today a cinematic aesthetic, created by individual directors, and independent of television, exists all over the world. The fact that television is involved in co-production – to a greater or lesser extent, depending on the country – that can't really influence these directors in their aesthetic. If they allow themselves to be influenced, that's their fault. At least it's possible for a director to make his film using money from television, yes, but without kowtowing to a television aesthetic. Guys like Antonioni and Godard, or like Herzog and Wenders and Kluge, they all make films that are more or less co-financed by television, and which use television as a reasonably effective screening medium – or, if you like, a feeble medium – for putting over subject matter, but one that in formal terms has nothing whatever to do with television aesthetic as I understand it.

   Yes, fewer films are made. And one strand of cinema is evolving into a kind of sensation-oriented cinema, which tends to be colossal and bombastic – yes, you can see that everywhere. But against that, you still get completely individual or completely national cinema, and that's far more important than the cinema that is indistinguishable from television.

WERNER HERZOG:
I think I'll start by taking my shoes off. You can't answer a question like that with your shoes on.

   I don't see the situation in the stark terms of the question. We aren't all that affected by television; film aesthetic is something apart and separate.

Telly is just a kind of jukebox: you're never enclosed within the space of the film itself the way you are in a cinema; you have a sort of mobile position as a viewer. And you can switch it off – you can't switch off a cinema.

I'm not all that worried. I was talking to a friend one night recently in New York. We went for a long walk and he told me how worried he was about everything being taken over by video and television. I expect you'll soon be able to choose vegetables in the supermarket by video camera and order your lunch by pressing buttons on your telephone or your computer. It probably won't be long till you can draw money out of the bank via video – or maybe you can do that already. I'm not so worried, I said to him, because whatever happens on television, life will be going on somewhere else.

Wherever life touches us most directly, that's where you'll find the cinema. And that's what'll survive. Nothing else.

ROBERT KRAMER:

I started off as a writer. I wrote novels, and I felt I was being shoehorned into an enormous tradition. The cinema offered me more freedom. There, there were no rules. That was my terrain. I could do what I wanted, just like the other film-makers. That's what cinema is.

Cinema is real. The books are on the shelves.

ANNA CAROLINA:

Every day I think of giving up film-making. If I could put together small productions, with energy and commitment . . . But instead I see the writer disappearing, and language and subject matter becoming *passé*.

The electronic film doesn't interest me, and it can't interest any genuine artist. I don't know what else to say.

MAHROUN BAGDADI:

The problem I have with the cinema, with the films I watch, with the directors I like and who affect my work, is this: how do you make a film without getting trapped in a vicious circle? A film is made from creativity, struggle and pain. But people who make films no longer take the time to live. Film-making overlaps with life to such an extent that you have to ask yourself: at what point am I putting my own life on the screen, or living out my own films?

STEVEN SPIELBERG:

I must be one of the last optimists, where the history and the future of the film industry in Hollywood is concerned. I even believe there will be an expansion of the cinema. I hope it won't be at the expense of other films. We all know that money's tight: it's 1982, and the purchasing power of the dollar isn't what it once was. In 1974, when I was making *Jaws* and went 100 days over on the shooting schedule – it went up from 55 to 155 days! – the film's budget rose to $8 million. Today, because of the dollar, the franc, the mark, the yen, whatever – there's world-wide inflation besetting the film industry – *Jaws* would probably cost $27 million. And a film like *E.T.* – at $10.3 million it's the cheapest movie I've made in the last two years – would cost about $18 million in five years' time. And that's a film set in a house. Back yard, front yard, a few shots in a forest, really very limited locations ...

I don't think we can pin the blame on anyone. We can't go and say it's all your fault – to the unions, who push up the budgets by 15 per cent every year in Hollywood, or the government, or the weak dollar. Of course it's no one's fault; it's the general economic climate. We should be satisfied with what we've got, and make the best films we can. If we compromise, and end up having to make a film for $3 million or $4 million when its budget ought to be more like $15 million, then we'll just have to do it. We are the captives of our times.

It appears that everyone in positions of power in Hollywood – those people in the studios with the power to say yes or no – wants a hit. They want an unstoppable thunderbolt in extra time in the final of the World Cup, with the score at four-all. Everyone wants to be a hero, and just before lights-out in Hollywood they want to take a piece of shit out of their desk drawer and turn it into a silk purse, and produce a last-minute hit, a $100 million hit. The studio bosses seem to think that if a film doesn't promise to be at least a hit, and preferably a blockbuster, they want to have nothing to do with it. That's the danger. It doesn't come from the film-makers or the producers or the writers. It comes from the people holding the purse-strings. They say I want to get my money back on this project, and I want it back tenfold. What I don't want to see is some film about your personal life, about your grandfather, about what it was like growing up in an American high school, what it was like jerking off when you were thirteen, or any of that crap. Got it? I want a film that will appeal to everyone.

In other words: Hollywood wants the ideal film that will suit every audience. And that, of course, is an impossibility.

MICHELANGELO ANTONIONI:
The cinema is in a parlous state, I agree. But we should look at the situation from more than one angle. The effect of television on attitudes and ways of seeing – children's especially – is undeniable. On the other hand, we should admit that the situation may seem particularly precarious to us, because we come from a different generation. So what we should really do is adapt ourselves to the future world and its modes of representation.

There are new forms of reproduction, new technologies like magnetic tape which will probably come to replace traditional film stock, which no longer meets today's requirements. For instance, Scorsese has pointed out that colour film fades over time. The problem of entertaining ever-larger audiences may be solved by electronic systems, by lasers, or by other technologies still being invented – who can say?

But, of course, I also worry about the future of film as we know it. Because it gave us so many ways of expressing what we felt and what we thought we had to say, we feel an immense gratitude to it. But the more we extend the range of technical possibilities, the more this feeling will diminish. There is always a dichotomy between the attitudes of today and those of a future we are still unable to imagine. Who knows what houses may look like in the future – those structures we see through the window opposite will probably no longer exist. We must turn our minds not to the immediate but to the distant future: to the condition of the world that will greet future generations.

I'm really quite optimistic. I've always tried to bring the latest expressive forms into my films. I've used video in one of them; I've experimented with colour, and literally painted reality. It was like a kind of crude proto-video technique. I'd like to try further experiments in that direction, because I'm sure that the possibilities of video will teach us different ways of thinking about ourselves.

It's difficult to talk about the future of the cinema. High-quality video cassettes will soon bring films into people's homes; cinemas will be used less. Current structures will disappear. Not as quickly and easily as that suggests, but it will happen, and we will be unable to prevent it. We can only try to get used to the idea.

In *Deserto Rosso* I examined the problem of adapting – adapting to new technologies, to new levels of pollution in the air we'll have to breathe. Our own organisms will evolve – who knows what lies in store for us. The future will present itself with unimaginable ruthlessness. That's really all I have to say; I'm neither a good speaker, nor a good abstract thinker. I'd sooner work practically and try things out than talk about them. My feeling is it won't be all that hard to turn us into new men, better adapted to our new technologies.

WIM WENDERS:
Yesterday I went to see another film-maker who was unable to come to this room. He is a Turk. The Turkish government has demanded his extradition and for that reason he couldn't leave the security of his place of refuge.

He has answered the same question concerning the future of the cinema, and recorded his reply. The speaker is Yilmaz Güney:

The cinema has two sides, industry and art, and one cannot be without the other. To reach the masses one must understand who they are and what they want. The industry must occupy itself with that, because consumer demands are continually changing. The task of the art of film is to follow socio-political developments, and follow the evolving consciousness of the public. Art tells stories to the public, industry wants to make its profits from the storytelling.

As soon as a young film-maker is required to work with capitalist producers, his independence is taken away from him. He is given set parameters to work within, and he becomes part of decadent cinema instead of continuing to represent hope. That's where the tragedy lies: the artist's and the cinema's.

May 1982

Film thieves
from a public discussion in Rome

The name given to this colloquium is '*Ladri di cinema*', film thieves, and it was my original plan to show excerpts from films which have influenced my work. I still think it's a good idea, but in the end I preferred to show one film in its entirety, Ozu's *Tokyo Monogatari*. I can't claim to have stolen anything from this film – perhaps I should have chosen another one instead; I've stolen plenty of things from American films, for example, but nothing from this one. It's easiest to steal from thieves, and Ozu is no thief. You can learn from him, but not pilfer things from him. The most important thing I learned from this film, and from all the others of his that I've seen, is this: that life itself is the greatest possible adventure for the cinema. I also learned that it makes no sense to try to force a story on a film. I've learned from Ozu that you can have a narrative film without a 'storyline'. You have to believe in the characters and allow them to arrive at a story about themselves. You shouldn't start with a story in mind and then look for appropriate characters; you must begin with the characters and, in collaboration with them, look for their story.

What are the difficulties in working with a fixed camera?
As you can see from Ozu's film, it's no problem. The choice between having a mobile or a fixed camera is a fundamental stylistic one. The term 'fixed camera' sounds so restrictive. It can be quite exhilarating.

Are your films concepts or visions?
For me, the cinema is primarily a form. A film must have a form, otherwise it doesn't say anything. 'Form' is something visual, not intellectual. When I'm making a film I look a lot, and think very little. You think later, during the editing, not while you're shooting.

Have you stolen anything from Antonioni's Blow Up?

Yes, I'm pretty sure I have. Not its 'style' or anything, but the odd detail from it. Anything is stealable, but if you steal too much the penalties are very high. I can say, for example, that I may have stolen the colour green from *Blow Up*. That colour existed before Antonioni's film, but that's where I first saw it.

Do you work on your scripts a lot?

Yes, but not in the usual way. Normally a script has to be finished before the shooting starts. What I do is to write like a lunatic every night during the filming; whatever I may have written before is just for the purpose of raising money. The script isn't the film. A film only gets its definitive impulse from the first day of filming, and what you have to do is to go with it, and try to guide it.

You've said that the story is built up from the characters, and the characters, presumably, are created from the encounter between direc-tor and actors. How does that relationship between actor, director and character take shape in your films?

The actor must be someone I have respect for, and not just because we're working on a film together. He must be someone whose story I'm eager to learn. The film is the product of our joint effort to use his biography in a story. An actor who accepts a part in a film is risking a lot. He must be prepared to lay himself open, to put himself at my mercy.

What are the differences between you and your colleagues in the New German Cinema?

The New German Cinema isn't a distinct category like Italian Neo-Realism or the French *Nouvelle Vague*. We don't have a certain kind of plot or a common style. What brought us together was just our need to make films again, in a country where that medium had been disrupted and discredited for years. From the outset, we were all very different as writers and directors, and that allowed us to respect one another and to feel solidarity with each other. Our solidarity was the source of the New German Cinema. If we'd been nationals of another country we might have been more inclined to envy one another. Nowadays we usually only meet in airport lounges, on our way to or returning from somewhere.

Why are there so many trains in your films?

Ozu has trains in almost all his films too. Once he was asked why and he said it was because he was so fond of them. The locomotive with all its wheels simply belongs to the cinema. It's a piece of machinery like the cine-camera. They are both products of the nineteenth century, the mechanical age. Trains are 'steam-cameras on rails'.

Why did you film The State of Things *in black and white?*

For me, black and white is reality in the cinema: it's the way you describe essences, rather than surfaces. Of course, it's perfectly legitimate for films to be about surfaces, but this film happens to be about essences. Sam Fuller, who plays the cameraman in the film, answers the question better than I can here.

Ozu is a cinéaste of interiors and you of open spaces. He uses long, static angles, your shots are continually in motion. How can you steal from him, where is there a resemblance?

Often the most exciting moments in Ozu's films are the rare scenes where he films out of doors. (I still have great admiration for his interiors, though.) For myself, I prefer filming outside because I don't think I have any special facility with interiors. Besides, it's not true that he uses long, static angles; he cuts a lot. And also the film we've just seen contains, in my opinion, the most beautiful tracking shots in all of cinema. It's true, I have too many tracking shots, but I hope that some time, when I'm older, I'll be able to make a film that just uses one or two. This is where the question of Ozu's style comes in; and that's where you realize you can't lift things from him, you can only hope to learn.

Do you go to the cinema much?

In bursts.

While I'm shooting I don't look at other films. And the rest of the time, I'll sometimes go every day. Often I'll just go and see whatever's playing, regardless, usually mediocre films. There's a lot you can steal there.

Your films are all road-movies, and the characters go on and on, without any particular destination in mind. Where are they going?

You're right, they're not going anywhere; or rather, it's not important to them to arrive anywhere particular. What's important is having the right 'attitude', to be moving. That's their aim: to be on the road. I'm like that myself too; I prefer 'travelling' to 'arriving'. The condition of motion is very important to me. If I've been too long in a place, I somehow get uncomfortable; I'm not saying I get bored, but I get the feeling I'm less open to stimuli than when I'm moving. The best way I've found of making films is moving on – my imagination works best under that condition. As soon as I've been too long in a place I can't think of any fresh images, I'm no longer free.

People often imagine that, by not going anywhere, my characters are missing out on something, a place to go to. In fact, the opposite is true: these characters have the good fortune of not *having* to go anywhere. I find it liberating, being able to go on without knowing where. Not to have a home to which one must return – I see that as a positive and attractive situation.

What is the role of memory in your films?

That's a nice title for a film, 'The Role of Memory'. Every film starts off from memories, and every film is also a sum of many memories. Then again, every film creates memories. The cinema itself has created many memories.

Nostalgia. There is something in your films that your characters are missing, a kind of security, of certainty. Do you think memory can be a substitute for security? And can film-making compensate for your own insecurity?

To my mind, insecurity is an excellent condition to be in. One shouldn't be in too much of a hurry to end it. I believe one can be happy, even if there are certain areas of insecurity in one's life. Insecurity, uncertainty, is certainly a way of prolonging one's curiosity. But perhaps I've misunderstood your question: what does insecurity have to do with nostalgia?

Perhaps the characters in your films have the feeling they are missing or have lost something, and are trying to regain it in their memories . . . ?

That's true. The characters in my films spend a lot of time being retrospective. Nostalgia is belonging to the past, feeling connected with the past. I don't think they exactly wish they *were* in the past, because there is no hope there. But every film begins as a memory or a dream, and dreams are a kind of memory. That's how they start off. But then, after that, you're out filming – that is, encountering a particular kind of reality. And there it's important to give the reality more weight than the dream.

In every film there is a conflict between the past and the future. And only what has actually been filmed finds a present, an equilibrium which never actually existed. I suppose my 'security' is there: making a film and looking at it, that's something you can 'hold on to'.

You've emphasized the difference between the landscape in your films and the landscape in classic German cinema. Could you tell us something about that difference?

Yes, 'classic' German films are always set in cities. I would say the feeling of German Expressionist cinema is claustrophobic in every way. The background for my own films, though, comes much more from the films I saw as a child, in particular Westerns, where the sun shines all the time. Have you ever seen a German film from the twenties that has brilliant sunshine in it?

For me, landscape has everything to do with cinema! The first time I had a real 16 mm camera in my hands, I did one three-minute take, because that's how long the reel was. It was of a landscape. I set up the camera; there was nothing happening. The wind blew, clouds passed overhead, nothing happened. It was an extension of painting for me, of landscape painting. I didn't want to put anyone in the foreground, and even today when I'm making a film I feel more interested in the sun rising over the landscape than in the story that's going on there: I feel greater responsibility for the landscape than for the story I've situated in it. I learned that from Western directors too, one of them in particular: Anthony Mann.

Can you imagine making a film with a woman as the central character?

All ten films I've made to date are a preparation for telling stories about men and women. They're just a prologue, the first steps to being able to talk about relationships. It seemed easier for me to begin with male relationships, especially in the seventies. But that was just a preparation for me, and I hope, after a few films, to take a step forward and start telling stories about men and women. But I don't want to tell them in the accustomed way: that tradition is so false, so horribly and vilely false, especially where the women are concerned. It's very rare for women to be well portrayed in the cinema. Only very few directors have managed it. Antonioni is one of them. I won't always be telling stories about men.

September 1982

Goodbye to the booming voice of the old cinema
from a conversation with Wolfram Schütte

I wanted to talk to you, not only about The State of Things, *but also about the situation of the cinema.*

In other words, the state of things again.

How did you come to choose that Sartrean title?

It's an old one. I started a film once with Robby Müller in the early seventies. The prints are still in the lab, but nothing ever came of it.

What do you understand by 'the state of things'? Have they stopped moving, is there stasis, or a 'false movement'?

The first use of the title in 1972 was for a totally phenomenological film. We wanted to make something that was purely descriptive. The title stayed with me; it was purely literal then. Today it's meant in a more metaphorical way. In the winter of 1981/2 I had a great deal of time to think; I was away from Hollywood for the first time in quite a while. It's such a closed system, you know. If you're there, in it, it's really difficult to see it with any perspective; there are all kinds of examples of that: people who were only able to realize what was happening there once they'd got out. It took me till then to come up with any kind of assessment of the situation: and I used that title. What I like about it is that the phrase exists, with the same meaning, in the three languages I know: German, English and French.

In The State of Things *you get a pretty clear view of the relationship between producer and director; but why (as you discover later) the scriptwriter has invested his own money in the film, and what it means to him in artistic terms – both of those questions are a little unclear.*

You have to understand that, however important the screenwriter is in the Hollywood set-up (because they only ever take on finished scripts) and however highly paid he is (you hear of $1 million being paid for a script, and writers are generally better paid than directors), his existence within the system remains deeply insecure and subordinate. I've met distinguished writers who were sacked overnight. They were told: 'We've got your book, so what do we need you for?' and the writer reads in the paper that someone else has been hired to work on his book. He's an employee, extremely well paid, but with no rights to his work. Script-writers are placated by money, but they occupy an uneasy space between producer and director. I had thought that Hollywood scriptwriters had safe jobs, and rather more power and influence than they actually have. Since that isn't the case, I made Dennis the shakiest figure in my film; having him actually invest his own money in his film is maybe a bit over the top but I actually know of Hollywood authors who did just that, to buy themselves a say in the production. There are so many writers – maybe one screenplay out of every hundred actually gets made – and the most important thing for these writers (there are really thousands of them hanging around there) is their first 'credit'. The quality of the film is strictly secondary. It's not until a writer has got his name up on the screen that he's in play. Until that time, he's nobody. And they fight for that like crazy, especially the young ones whom I saw a lot of; they'll do anything for that first 'credit', they'll kill their grandmothers. That's why Dennis has his own money in his own film.

How did you come to cast Paul Getty III in that part?

I'd known Paul for a couple of years by then; I knew him as someone who wasn't really sure about what he wanted, who was rather alienated from his background and his life. He came over to Portugal from Rome and asked if there was anything he could do. And since the part of the writer was still open, it seemed to me like a stroke of luck, and I think Paul was really, really good in the part. It was a risk, of course, working with someone who had no experience as an actor, but I think it really paid off.

Did you ever have it in mind to have a German actor play the director?

Yes, I'd offered the part to Hanns Zischler. He couldn't make it. Rüdiger Vogler had a theatre job in Paris, so he couldn't either. Then I asked Lou Castel, but he'd just signed up to do an Italian film; in fact it never went ahead, but it was too late by then. I would have liked to work with him.

Then I thought of Patrick Bauchau, who's been at the back of my mind for about ten years now because I thought he was wonderful in Eric Rohmer's *La Collectioneuse*. I kept asking myself: whatever happened to him? Then I heard that he'd stopped making films, had got out altogether and was working as a carpenter. Anyway, I got hold of him, and that was the next stroke of luck.

The director Friedrich says in The State of Things: *'I'm not at home anywhere . . .'*
That's a quote from Murnau . . .

. . . but where is home for this film, for yourself?
I think the film locates itself by pointing to – and enduring – the dialectical tension between the European and the American. As a film, it depicts both of these, and is itself somewhere in between. And clearly it gave me a vigorous and decisive push back towards the European cinema and my German past. However critical it is – and had to be – of the American cinema, it also has something positive to say about Gordon, the producer.

But Gordon's really a fossil . . .
Yes, but then it's a fossilized industry, not just the people in it but the way they think. It's amazing to me that this craft still exists in Hollywood, in that old-fashioned way. I don't think it's really any different now from what it was in the forties or fifties. Now as then, Hollywood is in the hands of a few people, the agents and the lawyers, and I don't think they do things any differently now from the way they did then. My own agent, for instance, went over there in the twenties, and it's the agents who have the most power there.

New Hollywood started out as a break with the old studio system. By now, though, it's all reverted to that same solid, investor-dominated system. What hope is there of being able to make films outside that great system, in an adventurous way?

Adventures always used to be possible, in the B-movies they made, in the films of Edgar Ulmer, and Howard Hawks and Preston Sturgess. The history of the Oscars is absolutely crazy. The films that got them, the mainstream productions of their day, are completely unknown now. The exciting films were always the little cheap ones. The big productions had to carry the message that the system wanted to hear, the message it paid its big budgets for: the success-story of America. The little films showed you the depression and the underside. They're not being made at the moment, or rather, they're coming back, one grade down, as C-movies.

Now, where B-movies are concerned, you knew what they were made for, namely for the cinema. Surely there isn't that same certainty now. You could say, with slight exaggeration, that the question today isn't why someone makes a film, but what's going to happen to it, where's it going to be shown?

Yes, a lot has fallen away and no longer exists. There are just a handful of titles on cinema programmes in the United States, and backing them up maybe another ten or a dozen that are a shade less successful. And these films play in every cinema from coast to coast. The role of the B-movie in this set-up has been taken over by European films, which have a considerable following in the 'art-houses', and, you know, there are whole chains of these 'art-houses' now: it's not just New York and San Francisco, but other cities too.

But you could never say the classic B-movie was 'art' . . .

Yes, that is an enormous change. Bear in mind, though, that most of what the B-movies catered for is now supplied by television, by the soaps. So perhaps another reason for their discontinuation is because television has taken over their function from the cinema, and the only thing the regular cinema now provides is the mammoth production number.

That's right. So then shouldn't The State of Things *have taken in television as well, to provide a full assessment of the condition of the cinema?*

Yes. But I only took in the cycle from production to distribution to cinema screening.

Films of yours like Lightning Over Water *(about the dying Nicholas Ray, the man and his films) or* The State of Things, *are meditations on cinema history, they are about making movies and living in and around them. But a sense of cinema history, of a living cinema tradition, exemplified by the names and works of Ray or Fuller or Fritz Lang, surely that's something that's conspicuously lacking in cinemagoers, particularly here in Germany. Is that something you can live with?*

That came out very clearly with *Lightning Over Water*. In Paris it got quite a decent response, but there was practically nothing here in Germany. That could also be to do with another problem, namely that in the Mediterranean countries the subject of death isn't taboo, the way it is in Germany. I hope *The State of Things* isn't involved with tradition to the extent that the German public turns its back on it.

I got the impression that what your director Friedrich does to his backers – i.e. protest against the way films are generally made in Hollywood – is what your film does as a whole. And yet audiences in the USA and over here go to see precisely those films that The State of Things *implicitly and explicitly opposes.*

Absolutely.

What are those stories that 'can no longer to told'? That constitutes a great part of the argument in The State of Things.

It was important to me to have Friedrich directing a remake. I wanted to say that stories that are merely based on other stories are inadmissible – or should be inadmissible. Stories whose only reality is the reality of the films in which they were previously used. For a long time now the bulk of what the cinema has had to offer has been more or less the remake. Hence the importance of the question of where the stories in films come from. My own film doesn't propose anything, doesn't state categorically: this story is OK, that one isn't. But the fact that the producer and director end up getting killed is really a clear signal that the thing they have in common – that style of cinema – is itself dead.

Why is it that the cinema doesn't come up with any new stories?

Lotte Eisner once told me that Fritz Lang asked her: why do you bother going to the cinema? You don't see any new films, everything is just being done over again.

Which is what he himself did in his last work.
Because it was the only way he could still earn a living in his profession. Since then it's become even bleaker than Lang could have imagined. Once the idiom of the cinema had been invented, it simply took off on its own and left behind its original purpose and function – namely to define reality, to produce and reflect the external world in a set form. That idea of the cinema – the reason for which I would say it was 'invented' – is lost. So now this (film) language reads nothing but itself.

Are you saying that a certain documentary aspect of the cinema has been lost . . .
Yes, if you like – although you could say exactly the same thing about the documentary film. It's in exactly the same dilemma.

Doesn't the wish to tell stories imply a patterning of experience, a concentrating of life? Telling stories isn't only interpreting, it's bringing order into things . . .
Exactly, and telling stories on film aims at recognition from the spectator while the form tries to produce order out of a chaos of impressions. Ever since Homer (whom I'm reading at the moment), mankind has needed stories to learn that coherence is possible. There is a need for connections, because human beings don't experience much coherence. Correspondingly, there is an inflationary surge of 'impressions'. I would say that the need for stories is actually greater because you have a narrator ordering experience and suggesting that you can actually take control of your own life. That's what stories do. They confirm your ability to determine the meaning of your life.

They assert that you have experienced something.
But most people aren't able to do that – telling a story is difficult – and instead they produce a sentence that I find incredibly sad. They say, 'I'll never forget that. I'll never forget that as long as I live.' They say it to enhance their experience, or to make up for their inability to relate it

properly. Actually what they mean is: 'I can't really tell it to you properly, but you know what I mean.' In other words, they've stopped trying to communicate.

When I see The State of Things, *it sometimes looks to me as though you're trying to depart from 'stories'. The American cinema you were so fond of was a storytelling cinema. And that's what this film now takes issue with. Would you say you were going back to an associative or situational cinema, something like Kluge . . . ?*

Well, that's the dilemma: all my stories are really little details, whether they're about cities or emotions or feeling lost. All of what I want to communicate – it's not stories. That happens in the film. Friedrich says: 'There are no more stories', and straightaway he experiences a proper story in his life. *The State of Things*, the way it was made, is another example of that. It was flying blind, it could have taken another course or shown something completely different. I'm pleased with what it did show me: the truth about 'stories'. The idea that cinema should be bound up with life and experience (my experience as a film-maker, as much as the experience of the viewer), that idea – as the film made clear to me – is indissolubly connected with stories. Films that have given up narrative and only depict situations are simply not possible for me. To convey everything you want to, you simply have to tell stories . . .

So is a story just the thread . . .?

No, no, it's more than that. A story brings in structure. The story in *The State of Things* could have been left as a thread if Friedrich had just left his producer riding around in his caravan: an open ending. But if I'd left it open like that, suspended, everything else I'd wanted to say would have been left equally up in the air. By making the story conclusive as opposed to inconclusive (by killing off the central figures), all the rest of it has also gained definition. So I've learned that I have to take on board story as structure, that I have to reacquire a dramaturgical language in order to be able to say everything else equally firmly. For a couple of weeks now I've been reading Homer and discovering why stories have to be affirmative; why you need a set form to be able to talk about things that aren't contained in the narrative. It's a paradox. You have to watch your stories; let them out of your sight for a moment, they're up and away – as you can see in current American cinema: they're only telling the affirmative type of story, its highlights, as a kind of lying stunt. Reduced to that, storytelling is just froth.

Why is there this plague of twice-told tales in the American cinema, all these remakes?

They've given up experiencing things – life – outside the cinema and as a result they're unable to get anything of that into their films. I read a very frank interview with Steven Spielberg. He said he thought it was a great loss to himself that his entire experience, his world, consisted entirely of his childhood cinema experiences. It's an astonishing admission, but I think he'll just carry on regardless. I don't believe he'll ever do anything different.

But – to return to this again – isn't that your subject too, most recently in The State of Things *and also in your earlier films – the cinema, and its effect on your life and work and sensibility?*

Up until now, yes. I would say, looking back, that there was something compulsive about it; it was a kind of alibi to permit me to tell any kind of story at all. Whatever story I told always began with this alibi. Hence these constant hints that I appreciate there is a language of film that's already been used to say this and that, etc. I see all that now as having been rather compulsive. That'll change.

But isn't it particularly important – now that a cinema of showing and telling is vanishing, forgetting its own traditions – to remember it and preserve it, and in a way keep faith with it? Or do you think it's time to say: forget all that, it's finished? Should one plunge into the new and do, say, video work?

One man has already been through that: Godard. You have to learn from what happened to him. He's back with us again now . . .

. . . not properly, though . . .

. . . no, not properly: perhaps he's neither one thing nor the other yet, perhaps his plight is even worse than ours here in Germany. I've gone on respecting this cinematic tradition, but now with *The State of Things* I've taken a pretty exposed position: the way the film ends, I'm compelled to show my alternative view of the cinema of today or the near future. Either I show that storytelling is once more possible, or I shut up. That's what I've set myself in my next two films. Try a narrative that passionately and confidently assumes the relevance of film language to life and is no longer at pains to relate the story to the method of storytelling. Not to leave everything to the great box-office spectaculars, but to proceed with full confidence and tell stories – without lamenting or looking back on the fine storytelling tradition the cinema used to have. Tell stories and not look back is what I want to do.

That sounds rather like what Peter Handke has in mind in the literary field. But is it possible to recover such innocence?

That's the big question. At least it won't return us to depersonalized and mythical narrative. That was the achievement of classic American cinema: the collective narrative that came out of the studio system. All the myths that related the cinema to the great narratives in other media were created by this collective narration. Neither the European film nor the 'auteur' movie ever managed that. None of us has been able to tell stories like that. Our stories were all subjective. Now we have to acknowledge that that collective narrative form isn't recoverable or imitable. We shouldn't go on lamenting the fact. It's finished. And yet there's this huge demand for story. People want to be shown coherence – not only in *Star Wars* but also in stories where they can recognize themselves. We must stop lamenting that the old booming-voiced cinema isn't around any more.

You made a film in Cannes in which you asked a number of your colleagues how they saw the future of the cinema. What would you say they came up with?

The most interesting views, I think, were Antonioni's. He said the cinema with wide screens and big stories was probably on the way out, but we shouldn't resign ourselves on account of that. The need for stories in pictures will keep on growing. We have to acquaint ourselves with new media, and try to find a form for them, instead of leaving everything to the big entertainment corporations. He took a positive attitude: keep on working and participating, try to keep influencing things, and be at the forefront of new developments. And then, when there's no film camera for me in a couple of years' time, he said, then I'll get involved in electronic images. He really impressed me.

To get back to storytelling again: television tells stories the whole time; but what distinguished the cinema is the space between the story, the characters or the things themselves.

My answer to that would be that there is an amazing number of rules attached to telling stories in the cinema but, in spite of that, cinema has always left more breathing space than television. In television these rules have tightened, just as the screen has shrunk. A clear example is when you watch films on TV. The spaces are no longer evident, say the wide shots in Westerns. The rules have to be tighter because the viewer has to be tied to the thing more tightly. The cinema always kept this wonderful distance. But that's changing too now. New American films are just like television in the way they tie you to the screen. The loose bonds are getting tighter all the time.

Yes, that's my impression too. They're trying to fill up the empty spaces in films with all kinds of ornamental bits and pieces, so that you're never just alone in front of the screen for a moment.

I keep having the physical sensation of being tied all the time – as though there were cables running from the screen to each seat. Like a dog on a leash, that's what it's like in the cinema nowadays; and I can understand a dog wanting to get free of its leash. Great cinema let people off their leashes. In John Ford's films, say, you were up there with the fellows on the screen in that great openness. Television keeps the leads tight, otherwise people would keep switching over.

So how would you describe a style of storytelling that doesn't either grab on to the old or adapt to the bad and constricting new? I would guess your film-stories might have something in common with Peter Handke's writings, which as you know have met with a mixed reception over here.

What Handke does is absolutely without precedent. Particularly in

Slow Homecoming. That's a book that's been badly misunderstood and hasn't had its due. There are experiences described in it for the first time; strands of consciousness it was thought impossible to describe in words. And the awful thing is that it was thought of as exotic, and people who grasped it were just dismissed as Handke freaks – people didn't realize what a crucial work it is for our whole civilization: a path through previously unknown terrain.

Weren't you going to make a film of it?

Yes, I wrote a screenplay – from *Slow Homecoming* to *The Scenic Route*, and I like it very much still.

Was that to be the film?

Yes, that was the film, but it was going to be pretty long, say three or four hours. The script committee (in the Ministry of the Interior) turned it down; we withdrew it ourselves from the Film Institute because we'd just heard these stupid noises coming out; and no one in television wanted to touch it. Everyone seemed to be saying: 'Wenders/Handke for Christ's sake!' It was the Interior Ministry people I felt most let down by, because they'd stuck their necks out before on *Kings of the Road* and *Alice in the Cities*. And it wasn't just a treatment that we'd submitted; it was a whole script, 180 pages long. I said to myself: I so badly want to tell a story now that I just can't go on battling with people for another year or so in the hope of getting the money together. So I had to put the project on a back burner.

What are you working on at the moment?

I'm hoping to make a film next January or February, for which we're trying to raise international funding as we did with *The State of Things*. There's a thirty-page treatment and it's based on a collection of short stories by the American writer Sam Shepard. He worked with Antonioni on *Zabriskie Point*; he's written a lot of stage plays and has been a movie actor too. I want to write the film with him. It'll be a thousand stories in one. We'll shoot it in Arizona or Texas.

Do the stories exist already?

Yes, the only question is how to link them – they're not just stories, but poems too, and little diary jottings. The whole thing is set in motels or on the road.

You mentioned two films.

The second one will be my biggest venture to date. It's called *The End of the Century*. It'll be shot in Germany and Australia. It's set in Australia at the turn of the millennium, 1999/2000. The main character is a biochemist who's done research on perception in the States, during the nineties. He has discovered a way of restoring the sight of blind people without touching their eyes. External stimuli are relayed into the brain's optic centres by electrochemical impulses. Then he turns the process round, as it were, projecting inner images and dreams on to screens. He makes a lot of progress on that, then he realizes what a weapon that would be: to be able to look inside people's minds. Because at the time the USA is a totalitarian state, he leaves and goes to the Australian desert with his family, his father and his grandfather; there he continues his research. His father and grandfather are both from Germany; he himself arrived in the USA as a little boy. It gives me the opportunity to show the history of three generations, because he's working with them in his research, on restoring their dream images, memories and childhood experiences. The scientist and his family survive a global nuclear catastrophe by tunnelling under a mountain. Perhaps they're the only survivors. His invention gives him the unique chance of preserving the history of our century through the memories of his father and grandfather. The film is half science fiction (the story of the man in the mountain) and half crystal images (video's out of date by then, so we'll have to think of something else). These crystal images show what he's been able to 'extract' from the minds of his father and grandfather. That'll be German history from the thirties to the year 2000. That'll be my biggest and most ambitious project.

November 1982

Impossible stories
Talk given at a colloquium on narrative technique

Where French and German each have a single word for it, English has only a two-part phrase: 'to tell stories'. That hints at my difficulty: the man you've invited to talk to you about telling stories is a man who over the years has had nothing but problems with stories.

Let me go back to the very beginning. Once I was a painter. What interested me was space; I painted cityscapes and landscapes. I became a film-maker when I realized that I wasn't getting anywhere as a painter. Painting lacked something, as did my individual paintings. It would have been too easy to say that they lacked life; I thought that what was missing was an understanding of time. So when I began filming, I thought of myself as a painter of space engaged on a quest for time. It never occurred to me that this search should be called 'storytelling'. I must have been very naïve. I thought filming was simple. I thought you only had to see something to be able to depict it, and I also thought a storyteller (and of course I wasn't one) had to listen first and speak afterwards. Making a film to me meant connecting all these things. That was a misconception, but before I straighten it out, there is something else I must talk about.

My stories all begin from pictures. When I started making my first film, I wanted to make 'landscape portraits'. My very first film, *Silver City*, contained ten shots of three minutes each; that was the length of a reel of 16 mm film. Each shot was of a cityscape. I didn't move the camera; nothing happened. The shots were like the paintings and watercolours I'd done previously, only in a different medium. However, there was one shot that was different: it was of an empty landscape with railway tracks; the camera was placed very close to these. I knew the train schedule. I began filming two minutes before one was due, and everything seemed to be exactly as it had been in all the other shots: a deserted scene. Except that two minutes later someone ran into shot from the right, jumped over the tracks just a couple of yards in front of the camera, and ran out of the left edge of the frame. The moment he disappeared, even more surprisingly, the train thundered into the picture, also from the right. (It couldn't be heard approaching, because there was no sync. sound, only music.) This tiny 'action' – man crosses tracks ahead of train – signals the beginning of a 'story'. What is wrong with the man? Is he being followed? Does he want to kill himself? Why is he in such a hurry? Etc., etc. I think it was from that moment that I became a storyteller. And from that moment all my difficulties began too, because it was the first time that something had happened in a scene I had set up.

After that, the problems came thick and fast. When I was cutting together the ten shots, I realized that after the shot where the man crosses the tracks hell for leather there would be the expectation that every subsequent shot would contain some action. So for the first time I had to consider the order of the shots, some kind of dramaturgy. My original idea, simply to run a series of fixed-frame shots, one after another, 'unconnected' and in no special order, became impossible. The assembling of scenes and their arrangement in an order was, it seemed already, a first step towards narrative. People would see entirely fanciful connections between scenes and interpret them as having narrative intentions. But that wasn't what I wanted. I was only combining time and space; but from that moment on, I was pressed into telling stories. From then on and until the present moment, I have felt an opposition between images and stories. A mutual incompatibility, a mutual undermining. I have always been more interested in pictures, and the fact that – as soon as you assemble them – they seem to want to tell a story, is still a problem for me today.

My stories start with places, cities, landscapes and roads. A map is like a screenplay to me. When I look at a road, for example, I begin to ask myself what kind of thing might happen on it; similarly with a building, like my own hotel room here in Livorno: I look out of the window, it's raining hard and a car stops in front of the hotel. A man gets out of it and looks around. Then he starts walking down the road, without an umbrella, in spite of the rain. My head starts working on a story right away, because I want to know where he's going, what kind of street he might be turning into.

Of course stories can also begin in other ways. Recently the following happened to me: I'm sitting alone in a hotel lobby, waiting to be collected by someone I don't know. A woman comes in, looking for someone *she* doesn't know. She comes up to me and asks: 'Excuse me, are you Mr So-and-so?' And I very nearly say 'Yes!' Just because I'm fascinated by the thought of experiencing the beginning of a story or a film. So it's possible that a story can be sparked off by a moment of drama, but usually it begins in contemplation, when I'm looking at landscapes, houses, roads and pictures.

For a writer, a story seems to be the logical end-product: words want to form sentences, and the sentences want to stand in some continuous discourse; a writer doesn't have to force the words into a sentence or the sentences into a story. There seems to be a kind of inevitability in the way stories come to be told. In films – or at least in my films, because of course there are other ways of going about it – in films the images don't necessarily lead to anything else; they stand on their own. I think a picture stands on its own more readily, whereas a word tends to seek the context of a story. For me, images don't automatically lend themselves to be part of a story. If they're to function in the way that words and sentences do, they have to be 'forced' – that is, I have to manipulate them.

My thesis is that for me as a film-maker, narrative involves forcing the images in some way. Sometimes this manipulation becomes narrative art, but not necessarily. Often enough, the result is only abused pictures.

I dislike the manipulation that's necessary to press all the images of a film into one story; it's very harmful for the images because it tends to drain them of their 'life'. In the relationship between story and image, I see the story as a kind of vampire, trying to suck all the blood from an image. Images are acutely sensitive; like snails they shrink back when you touch their horns. They don't have it in them to be carthorses: carrying and transporting messages or significance or intention or a moral. But that's precisely what a story wants from them.

So far everything seems to have spoken out against story, as though it were the enemy. But of course stories are very exciting; they are powerful and important for mankind. They give people what they want, on a very profound level – more than merely amusement or entertainment or suspense. People's primary requirement is that some kind of coherence be provided. Stories give people the feeling that there is meaning, that there is ultimately an order lurking behind the incredible confusion of appearances and phenomena that surrounds them. This order is what people require more than anything else; yes, I would almost say that the notion of order or story is connected with the godhead. Stories are substitutes for God. Or maybe the other way round.

For myself – and hence my problems with story – I incline to believe in chaos, in the inexplicable complexity of the events around me. Basically, I think that individual situations are unrelated to each other, and my experience seems to consist entirely of individual situations; I've never yet been involved in a story with a beginning, middle and end. For someone who tells stories this is positively sinful, but I must confess that I have yet to experience a story. I think stories are actually lies. But they are incredibly important to our survival. Their artificial structure helps us to overcome our worst fears: that there is no God; that we are nothing but tiny fluctuating particles with perception and consciousness, but lost in a universe that remains altogether beyond our conception. By producing coherence, stories make life bearable and combat fears. That's why children like to hear stories at bedtime. That's why the Bible is one long storybook, and why stories should always end happily.

Of course the stories in my films also work as a means of ordering the images. Without stories, the images that interest me would threaten to lose themselves and seem purely arbitrary.

For this reason, film-stories are like routes. A map is the most exciting thing in the world for me; when I see a map, I immediately feel restless, especially when it's of a country or city where I've never been. I look at all the names and I want to know the things they refer to, the cities of a country, the streets of a city. When I look at a map, it turns into an allegory for the whole of life. The only thing that makes it bearable is to try to mark out a route, and follow it through the city or country. Stories do just that: they become your roads in a strange land, where but for them, you might go to thousands of places without ever arriving anywhere.

What are the stories that are told in my films? There are two sorts; I draw a sharp distinction between them, because they exist in two completely separate systems or traditions. Furthermore, there is a continual alternation between the two categories of film, with a single exception, *The Scarlet Letter*, and that was a mistake.

In the first group (A) all the films are in black and white, except for *Nick's Film*, which belongs to neither tradition. (I'm not even sure that it counts as a film at all, so let's leave that one out.) In the other group (B) all the films are in colour, and they are all based on published novels. The films in group A, on the other hand, are based without exception on ideas of mine – the word 'idea' is used loosely to refer to dreams, daydreams and experiences of all kinds. All the A-films were more or less unscripted, whereas the others followed scripts very closely. The A-films are loosely structured, whereas the B-films are all tightly structured. The A-films were all shot in chronological sequence, beginning from an initial situation that was often the only known point in them; the B-films were shot in the traditional hopping-around way, and with an eye to the exigencies of a production team. With group A films, I never knew how they would finish; I knew the endings of B-films before I started.

Basically all the group A films operate in a very open system, the B-films in a very closed one. Both represent not only systems but also attitudes: openness on the one hand, discipline on the other. The themes of the A-films were identified only during shooting. The themes of the B-films were known; it was just a matter of deciding which bits should go in. The A-films were made from the inside, working out; the B-films the opposite. For the A-films a story had to be found; for the B-films the story had to be lost sight of.

The fact that – with the exception of the already-mentioned mistake – there has been a constant pendulum swing between A- and B-films shows that each film is a reaction to its predecessor, which is exactly my dilemma.

I made each of my A-films because the film before had had too many rules, hadn't been sufficiently spontaneous, and I'd got bored with the characters; also I felt that I had to 'expose' myself and the crew and the actors to a new situation. With the B-films it was exactly the other way round: I made them because I was unhappy that the film before had been so 'subjective', and because I needed to work within a firm structure, using the framework of a story. Actors in the B-films played parts 'other' than themselves, represented fictional characters; in the A-films they interpreted and depicted themselves, they *were* themselves. In these films I saw my task as bringing in as much as possible of what (already) existed. For the B-films, things had to be invented. It became ever clearer that one group could be called 'subjective' and the other 'search for objectivity'. Though, of course, it wasn't quite so simple.

In what follows I will talk about how the A-films began, and the role that story played in them. My first film was called *Summer in the City*; it's about a man who's spent a couple of years in prison. The first frame shows him emerging from prison and suddenly confronting life again. He tries to see his old friends and get into his old relationships, but he quickly realizes that nothing can be the way it was before. In the end he takes off and emigrates to America. The second film in the A-group, *Alice in the Cities*, is about a man who's supposed to be writing a feature about America. He can't do it, and the film begins with his decision to return to Europe. He happens to meet a little girl, Alice, and her mother, and promises to take her back to her grandmother in Europe. Only he doesn't know where she lives; all he has is a photograph of the house. The remainder of the film is taken up by the search for the house.

A man tries to kill himself – that's how *Kings of the Road* starts. By chance, there's another man watching, so he gives up his kamikaze behaviour. The other man is a truck-driver. They decide to travel together – pure chance, again. The film is about their journey and whether the two have anything to say to each other or not.

The last of the A-films, *The State of Things*, is about a film crew who have to stop working because the money's run out and the producer's vanished. The crew don't know whether they'll be able to finish the shoot or not. The film is about a group of people who've lost their way, particularly the director, who in the end goes to Hollywood to look for the producer.

All these films are about people who encounter unfamiliar situations on the road; all of them are to do with seeing and perception, about people who suddenly have to take a different view of things.

To be as specific about this as I can, I'd like to go back to *Kings of the Road*. How did that come about? One answer would be: because I'd just finished *False Movement* – it was a reaction to that previous work. I felt that I had to devise a story in which I could investigate myself and my country – Germany (the subject of my previous film too, though treated in a different way). This time it was to be a trip to an unknown country, to an unknown country in myself, and in the middle of Germany. I knew what I wanted but I didn't know how to begin. Then everything was set off by an image.

I was overtaking a truck on the Autobahn; it was very hot and it was an old lorry without air-conditioning. There were two men in the cab, and the driver had opened the door and was dangling his leg out in order to cool off. This image, seen from the corner of my eye when driving past, impressed me. I happened to stop at a motorway caff where the lorry also stopped. I went up to the bar where the two men from the lorry were standing. Not a word passed between them; it was as though they had absolutely nothing in common. You got the impression they were strangers. I asked myself what do these two men see, how do they see, as they drive across Germany?

At that time I was doing quite a lot of travelling around Germany with my previous film, *False Movement*. During my travels I became aware of the situation of the rural cinema. The halls, the projection booths and the projectionists all fascinated me. Then I looked at a map of Germany and I realized there was one route down through it that I barely knew. It ran along the border between the GDR and the FRG; not only down the middle of Germany, but also along the very edge. And I suddenly realized that I had everything I needed for my new film: a route and the story of two men who don't know each other. I was interested to see what might happen to them, and between them. One of them would have a job that was something to do with the cinema, and I knew where the cinemas were to be found: along the border.

Of course that's not enough to make a story. All the films in the A-group started off with a few situations that I hoped might develop into a story. To assist that development, I followed the method of 'day-dreaming'. Story always assumes control, it knows its course, it knows what matters, it knows where it begins and ends. Daydream is quite different; it doesn't have that 'dramaturgical' control. What it has is a kind of subconscious guide who wants to get on, no matter where; every dream is going somewhere, but who can say where that is? Something in the subconscious knows, but you can only discover it if you let it take its course, and that's what I attempted in all these films. The English word 'drifting' expresses it very well. Not the shortest line between two points, but a zigzag. Perhaps a better word would be 'meander', because that has the idea of distance in it as well.

A journey is an adventure in space and time. Adventure, space and time – all three are involved. Stories and journeys have them in common. A journey is always accompanied by curiosity about the unknown; it creates expectations and intensity of perception: you see things on the road that you never would at home. To get back to *Kings of the Road*: after ten weeks' filming we were still only halfway through, though I'd aimed to finish the film in that time. There was no money to go on filming, and we were still a long way short of an ending. The problem was: how should the journey end? Or: how might it be converted into a story? At first I thought of an accident. If it had been shot in America, it would certainly have finished with an accident. But thank God we weren't in America; we were free to do otherwise and get to the 'truth of our story'. So we broke off the filming and I tried to raise money for another five weeks' shooting. Of course a film of that type can be literally neverending, and that's a danger. The solution, finally, turned out to be that the men would have to realize they couldn't go on like that; a break had to come and they would have to change their lives.

But before that I had another idea, another 'bend' in the meander: the two protagonists look for their parents. I thought that might lead them to break off their relationship. So we filmed a long story about the first of them, how he visits his father, and then another long story about the second returning to the place where he grew up with his mother. Unfortunately, though, that only improved their relationship and left us even further from an ending than we were before. Suddenly, and for the first time, the two were able to speak to each other. We broke off the filming a second time. I thought the film might end with them both questioning what they had done before their relationship, and reconsidering their aims in life. The one travelling from cinema to cinema wonders whether there was any sense in keeping these places going, and the other goes back to his work as a paediatrician and speech therapist. In the end, that was how we shot it.

The State of Things is also about stories. Of course the director figure represents my own dilemma, to a certain extent; at one stage he actually says: 'Life and stories are mutually incompatible.' That's his theory as a director. Later on, though, when he goes back to Hollywood, he himself becomes embroiled in a story, in one of those stories he never believed in, and in the end it kills him. Paradoxical, of course. And that's really the only thing I have to say about stories: they are one huge, impossible paradox! I totally reject stories, because for me they only bring out lies, nothing but lies, and the biggest lie is that they show coherence where there is none. Then again, our need for these lies is so consuming that it's completely pointless to fight them and to put together a sequence of images without a story – without the lie of a story. Stories are impossible, but it's impossible to live without them.

That's the mess I'm in.

1982

Tokyo-Ga

If our century still had any shrines ... if there were any relics of the cinema, then for me it would have to be the corpus of the Japanese director Yasujiro Ozu. He made fifty-four films in all, silents in the twenties, black-and-white films in the thirties and forties, and finally colour films until his death in 1963 – on 12 December, his sixtieth birthday.

Ozu's films always tell the same simple stories, of the same people, in the same city of Tokyo. They are told with extreme economy, reduced to their barest essentials. They show how life has changed in Japan over forty years. Ozu's films show the slow decline of the Japanese family and the collapse of national identity. They don't do it by pointing aghast at the new, American, occidental influences, but by lamenting the losses with a gentle melancholy as they occur.

His films may be thoroughly Japanese, but they are also absolutely universal. I have seen all the families in the world in them, including my parents, my brother and myself. Never before or since has the cinema been so close to its true purpose: to give an image of man in the twentieth century, a true, valid and useful image, in which he can not only recognize himself, but from which he can learn as well.

Ozu's work doesn't need my praise. In any case, a 'relic' of the cinema could only exist in an imaginary world. My journey to Tokyo was no sort of pilgrimage. I wondered whether I could still detect any traces of the time, whether there was anything left of that work, images or even people, or if too much had changed in Tokyo and in Japan in the twenty years since Ozu's death, and it was all irrecoverable.

I no longer have the slightest recollection.

I recollect nothing whatsoever.

I know I was in Tokyo.

I know it was in the spring of 1983.

I know.

I had a camera with me and did some filming. I have the pictures, they have become my memory. But I think to myself: if you'd gone there without a camera, you would remember more.

There was a film shown on the aeroplane, and as always I tried not to look at it, and as always I had to watch. Without sound, the pictures on the little screen looked even more vapid. A hollow form, a deception, a forgery of emotion.

Just looking out of the window did me good. If only it were possible to film like that, I thought, the way you sometimes open your eyes. Just looking, not trying to prove anything.

Tokyo was like a dream, and my own pictures of it look like something fantastic to me today. It's like finding a bit of paper on which you scribbled down what you dreamed as it got light outside: you read it in utter bewilderment, none of the scenes in it are familiar, it's like someone else's dream. So now it appears incredible to me that on my very first stroll I actually found this graveyard with groups of men sitting under blossoming cherry trees, picnicking, laughing and drinking. People were taking photographs all over the place, and the croak of ravens sounded in my ears long afterwards.

It wasn't till I saw this little boy on the underground, who'd simply had enough, that I realized why my images of Tokyo felt to me like the perceptions of a somnambulist: long before I ever went there, I had this very strong preconceived image of Tokyo and its inhabitants, more so than any other place on earth: it came from Ozu's films. No other city and its people have ever been so near and so familiar to me. I was trying to find this nearness myself, and it was that intimacy that my scenes from Tokyo were looking for. In the little boy on the underground I'd recognized one of the countless rebellious children of Ozu's films: or rather, I thought I had. Perhaps I was looking for something that no longer existed.

Until late that night, and then on every ensuing night, I lost myself in the deafening din of one of the innumerable *pachinko* halls, where you sit, alone in a crowd, in front of a machine, your eye following the metal balls threading their way among nails, usually going Out, and only very rarely finding their way into one of the winning areas. The game has a kind of hypnotic effect; it gives you a peculiar feeling of happiness. What you stand to win is negligible, except that time passes, and for a while you were lost to yourself and felt at one with the machine, able to forget whatever it was you wanted to forget. The game only became popular after the Second World War, when there was a national trauma for the Japanese to forget. Only the most adroit or the most fortunate, and, of course, the professional players, are able to increase their number of balls significantly and trade them in afterwards for cigarettes, food, electronic gadgets or tokens, which you can change illegally for cash in the surrounding backstreets.

The taxi back to the hotel. For a little extra on the bill, you can get a television and still more din for the ears and eyes. The more the reality of Tokyo appeared as a wanton, loveless, menacing, even inhuman proliferation of images, the greater and more potent was the lovingly ordered mythical city of Tokyo in the films of Yasujiro Ozu, in my memory. Perhaps it was no longer possible: a perspective able to order an ever more terrible world, a perspective that could still produce transparency. Perhaps that would be more than an Ozu of today could manage. Perhaps the hectic inflation of images has already destroyed too much. Perhaps images that can unite the world, and are at one with the world, perhaps they are gone for ever.

After John Wayne, it wasn't the stars and stripes that appeared, but the red circle of the Japanese flag, and as I dropped off, already half asleep, I thought: where I am is the centre of the world. Every fucking telly is the centre of the world. The centre has become a pathetic notion, and so has the image of the world become a pathetic idea, the more televisions there are in the world. Down with television.

We took a train to a nearby graveyard where Ozu lies buried. Kita Kamakura. The station appears in one of his own films.

There is no name on Ozu's gravestone, only an ancient Chinese character, MU, meaning 'nothingness'.

Going back on the train, I thought about that character. 'Nothingness'. I'd often tried to imagine it as a child. The idea had terrified me. Nothingness couldn't exist, I kept saying to myself. Only what was there could exist, reality.

'Reality'. There's probably no more hollow and useless idea than that, in connection with the cinema. Everyone knows what the perception of reality means. Everyone sees reality with his own eyes. You see others, especially the people dear to you, the things around you, the cities and landscapes you live in, you see death, the mortality of man and the transience of things, you see and you experience love, loneliness, happiness, sorrow, fear: everyone sees 'life' for himself.

People are by now so used to the wide gulf between the cinema and life that it makes you sit up and catch your breath when you see something true or real happening on the screen, even if it's just a child's gesture in the background, or a bird flying across the screen, or a cloud casting its shadow over the picture momentarily. It's become a rarity in today's cinema for such moments of truth to take place, for people and things to show themselves as they are.

That was the remarkable thing about Ozu's films, and his later films in particular: they had these moments of truth, no, they were great expanses of truth, from the first scene to the last, films that were actually and continually about life, and in which people, things, cities and landscapes all revealed themselves. Such a depiction of reality, such an art, no longer exists in the cinema. That's finished. MU, nothingness. Which is now.

Back in Tokyo, the *pachinko* halls were already shut. Only the Kogi-chi, the 'nailer', was still at work. Tomorrow all the balls would take a different course and a machine you won on today would tomorrow drive you to despair.

Later at night, in Shinjuku, a part of Tokyo that's wall-to-wall bars. In Ozu's films there are many such streets, where his lonely and abandoned fathers get drunk.

I set up my camera and shot the way I was used to; and then I did it again: the same street, from the same place, only using a different focal lens, a 50, which Ozu used for all his work. The result was a completely different scene, one that was no longer mine.

The next morning, the same invisible ravens cawed in the graveyard; children were playing baseball. On the roofs of the city skyscrapers the grown-ups were playing golf, an absolute craze in Japan, even if only a small minority ever gets the chance to play on a real golf course.

In some of Ozu's films, this craze is shown with some irony. But I was still astonished to see it demonstrated, as a balletic exercise, for the beauty and perfection of the movement. The point of the game, pushing the ball into a hole, seemed to have fallen into disrepute. I came across only one last solitary advocate of the practice.

I left the great clattering golf stadium for a quick supper. As always you could see a display of what dishes were available in the window of the restaurant. Afterwards, I returned to the now floodlit stadium.

Back in the club house later that night, images of baseball brought the day to a symmetrical conclusion. And because here too they had the same model food, I decided to go along the next day and look at one of the workshops where these very realistic dummy meals were made.

It all starts with genuine food. Then gelatine is poured over it and allowed to set. The moulds thus created are filled with wax, and these wax shapes are then trimmed, painted and refined. The wax has to be kept constantly warm. In other respects the preparation of a wax sandwich wasn't that dissimilar to the preparation of a real one.

I spent the whole day there. Only I wasn't allowed to film at lunchtime, which was a pity. The employees sat surrounded by wax artefacts and ate packed lunches which looked just like the imitations. You were afraid someone might take a bite out of a wax sandwich by mistake.

On Tokyo Tower I ran into my friend Werner Herzog, who was stopping over in Japan for a couple of days *en route* for Australia. We talked.

Werner Herzog:

'The simple truth is that there aren't many images around now.

'When I look out of the window here, everything is blocked up, images are almost impossible. You practically have to start digging for them like an archaeologist to try to find something in this damaged landscape. Of course there are often risks associated with that, but I'm not afraid. As I see it there are so few people left in the world prepared to do something for our plight, which is a lack of decent images. We urgently need images to accord with the state of our civilization, and with our own innermost souls.

'If you have to, you just go into the middle of a war, or wherever you have to go for them. I would never complain that it was too difficult, that you had to climb 27,000 feet up a mountain to get images that are still pure and clear and transparent.

'There's hardly anything left. You have to really look.

'I'd fly to Mars or Saturn on the next rocket if they'd take me. There's a NASA programme with that Skylab shuttle, where they'll perhaps take biologists or technicians up into space.

'I'd love to be there with a camera, because it's no longer easy to find things on earth to provide clarity in images as they used to exist. I would go anywhere.'

However much I sympathized with Werner's longing for clear and pure images, the images I was looking for existed only here on earth, in the tumultuous city. In spite of everything, I couldn't help being very impressed by Tokyo.

1983/4

Like flying blind without instruments
On the turning point in *Paris, Texas*

The story's about a man who turns up somewhere in the desert out of nowhere and returns to civilization. Prior to filming, we drove the length of the entire US–Mexican border – more than 1,500 miles. Finally we decided to shoot in an area called 'Big Bend' in the south-west of Texas. Big Bend is a National Park with incredibly beautiful mountains, through which the Rio Grande flows. That's the river the 'wetbacks' have to swim. As it turned out, we didn't film there, because when we were looking over the area again from above, in a helicopter, the old pilot, a local guy, told us there was an area a little way off called 'the Devil's Graveyard'. This godforsaken patch of ground wasn't even entered on our maps, and it turned out to be a gigantic abstract dream landscape. There are no police and most of the immigrants who swim across there just die in the desert because there's not a drop of water anywhere in it. So that's where we started our film; that's where we see Travis for the first time. After he collapses with exhaustion, he's picked up by his brother. The first place they go is a little hamlet of about twenty houses called Marathon. It has a hotel where Walt drops Travis, and goes off to buy him some new clothes. But when Walt gets back, his brother has taken off again. The next, slightly bigger, place that Walt and Travis pass through on their way from Texas to Los Angeles is Fort Stanton, a town with a couple of thousand inhabitants. We tried to arrange the film in such a way that all sizes and types of American towns appear in it.

Actually the smallest place of all was the gas station where Travis collapses. It was called Camellot, and we only stopped there on the recce because we thought it was a funny name. Then came Marathon, then Fort Stanton, then El Paso which is a middle-sized town, and finally the metropolis Los Angeles. I didn't show Los Angeles as a city, but as an enormous suburb. You don't really get to see 'LA' in the film. The only real city you see is Houston, Texas. Houston is one of my favourite cities in America. So, you see, I tried to show all kinds of towns, though of course there are also a lot of scenes that are just set in the countryside.

Actually, I was going to make a far more complex film, because I'd originally intended to drive all over America. I had it in mind to go to Alaska and then the Midwest and across to California and then down to Texas. I'd planned a real zigzag route all over America. But my scriptwriter Sam Shepard persuaded me not to. He said: 'Don't bother with all that zigzagging. You can find the whole of America in the one state of Texas.' At the time I didn't know Texas all that well, but I trusted Sam. I travelled around Texas for a couple of months, and I had to agree with him. Everything I wanted to have in my film was there in Texas – America in miniature.

A lot of my films start off with roadmaps instead of scripts. Sometimes it feels like flying blind without instruments. You fly all night and in the morning you arrive somewhere. That is: you have to try to make a landing somewhere so the film can end.

For me this film has come off better than, or differently to, my previous films. Once more, we flew all night without instruments, but this time we landed exactly where we meant to. From the outset, *Paris, Texas* had a much straighter trajectory and a much more precise destination. And from the beginning, too, it had more of a story than my earlier films, and I wanted to tell that story till I dropped.

May 1984

The growth of a small dependency
On the dispute with the Filmverlag der Autoren

It's a real struggle for me to confront this whole 'Filmverlag der Autoren versus *Paris, Texas*' business again. I'd hoped so much it might have resolved itself. I can't bear it any more, I can't stand it. All I can do, with the bit of anger and the bit of humour I've got left in me, is to say a few explanatory sentences under a few headings.

More than anything, I want my film to be shown in German cinemas; it's on all over the world, only not here, where I live. That hurts. I'm proud of it. That's why I haven't been able to agree to its being distributed by people who misjudge it or can't understand it or don't like it. It's my right, it must be my right. Painters can change galleries and footballers can get transfers to other teams.

Football

The Filmverlag der Autoren is, if you like, the team I don't want to play for any more, because they play with a ten-man defence. I'm one of the eponymous 'authors' who founded the company fourteen years ago and they've brought out all my films since then. But times have changed and the idea of a co-operative and of solidarity between authors has gone out of the window. The Filmverlag der Autoren is in no way different from the other commercial distributors.

Anyway: my new club is Tobis-Filmkunst. They play an attacking game and no offside trap. But, to stay with the metaphor, from the moment that offers started coming in from other distributors, my transfer fee kept getting pushed up, the way it is when there's a player who's 'unsettled' but his club doesn't want him scoring goals for other teams. And now, when he's become thoroughly pissed off, he learns he's got to go on playing for his original team.

Elephant and Mouse

We always used to set everything out openly on the table. The money never really bothered us that much. The people who say different are people who can't think of anything else anyway. We were bothered about just one thing: an appropriate evaluation of the film – and the distributor never came up with that. We had proposals and we were willing to move on all matters under dispute. The only (!) point that we weren't prepared to accept was the distributor's demand that the partner Wenders 'unconditionally' leave the company. In fact I am prepared to take such a step, but only after checking through the books. I'm not rich, and if resigning under those conditions were to cost me several hundred thousand marks, that would be financial suicide. Even so, we were always ready to talk about anything. But the elephant distribution company wasn't interested in what the mouse production company had to say. He was afraid of having his leg peed on.

Rudolf Augstein is a man I like and respect. When I refer here to 'distributors' or film publishers', I'm not referring to Rudolf Augstein. It's absolutely idiotic that things should have come to such a pass. I think he's quite as much a victim of what's going on as my film and me. When the two of us agreed a few weeks ago to come to an amicable settlement, I was grateful to Rudolf Augstein. I knew he meant it. The fact that our talks, after apparently producing agreement on the significant issues, were suddenly broken off by the other side without explanation – beyond the distributor now saying he did not want to go on distributing the film after all – that, in my opinion, was caused by the people conducting the discussions not telling Rudolf Augstein the truth, and never having any interest in either the film or an 'amicable' settlement, but only being out for power and revenge. I can't help feeling that the mouse was somehow to be punished. The issue wasn't the film, but the elephant's offendedness.

Dosh

The film *Paris, Texas* cost exactly 5 million and 51 marks. Our company, Road Movies, organized finance from West Germany, France and England, and was solely liable for all the risks and the overspend. The distributor had chipped in 300,000 marks (i.e. the Bundesfilmpreis for *The State of Things*) via its own production company, Projekt, as a German internal co-production. That corresponds to about one-seventeenth of the budget. In addition, the distributor advanced a guarantee of 200,000 marks. As that was for the German distribution rights, it doesn't count as co-production money.

During the course of the production, the Filmverlag lent us another 275,000 marks. This was an interim loan, which was guaranteed in full by the final instalments of money from the WDR (75,000 marks) and the Ministry of the Interior (200,000 marks). Even so, for this comparatively small part of the overall budget, the Filmverlag acquired a great deal in return: one-third of the producer's profits, and two-thirds of any awards from the exploitation of the film.

Such a state of affairs, in which the producer is so readily fleeced by the distributor, is typical of the present economic condition of the New German Film. In spite of its worldwide reputation and recent commercial success, there is no organization in Germany that will support its ventures morally and economically. Whereas the film industry in France embraced the *Nouvelle Vague* enthusiastically – and was itself completely reformed and financially regenerated as a result – nothing of the sort has happened over here.

Short and Curlies

The New German Film, dismissed originally as the work of a bunch of beginners, still has no roots in the German industry. Instead, stimulated by grants and TV co-production money, a whole clutch of under-capitalized little companies have sprung up. They flirt with bankruptcy every time they make a film, and, indeed, a lot of these companies have gone broke in the last few years. The distributors – the Filmverlag der Autoren among them – have taken advantage of their weak liquidity to acquire for relatively small guarantees and loans quite disproportionate shares in the rights to their films, bringing potential profit and power.

Road Movies is a case in point. When we ran out of money during the filming of *The State of Things* and needed a small loan to finish the film, we were forced to sign a contract for a minimal distribution guarantee, by which the Filmverlag der Autoren would acquire all the subsidies for the film, thus including the Bundesfilmpreis of 300,000 marks. That, in turn, funded their co-production involvement in *Paris, Texas*. In the course of just two films, a small dependence had become a great big one. The elephant had the mouse by the short and curlies.

This brings us to the really threatening point of the whole saga. On the basis of a possibly unethical bankruptcy clause, the distributors would acquire all rights to *Paris, Texas* in the event that Road Movies ever became insolvent – which is perfectly possible if all outstanding claims on us were presented at once. I can only see this as a piece of deliberate speculation on the part of the Filmverlag, in view of the way it has behaved with us over the last few weeks. That really would confirm that it was never the film they cared about, but power over us.

If things continue like this, there will soon be no German cinema and no producers, only distributors. No mice, only elephants. And the 'mammoths' over in Hollywood would laugh all the way to the bank.

This text appeared, together with a reply from Rudolf Augstein and a commentary from Peter Buchka, in the Süddeutsche Zeitung *on 14 December 1984.*

Two months later, shortly before the opening of the court hearing, the Berlinale number of the Berlin magazine tip *printed the following statement:*

'On the screen at last' was the distributors' slogan, and it will have made a lot of people think the dispute over *Paris, Texas* has been settled. Perhaps many of them thought the whole argy-bargy was just clever publicity anyway. God knows, it wasn't.

What it was actually about will be revealed in the court case due to come up before the Berlin Regional Court on 21 February 1985, which I've been awaiting impatiently for months. 'On the screen at last' may be what the distributors say, the so-called 'Authors' publishing company, which has succeeded in getting its way after a ruthless and baseless struggle through summary hearings and preliminary injunctions.

For myself I prefer to say: 'In the courts at last.' At last a hope of some light on this whole shady affair, and a chance to explain what it was all about. A chance to get at the truth, even perhaps justice. So what was it about?

The quarrel is between a production company and a distributor. The bone of contention was the film *Paris, Texas*. There's enough dishonesty in the movie business anyway; what with the lying and cheating and skulduggery, plenty of people wake up to find they've been sold down the river. That's the way it is. That's the way we were treated too, but that on its own wouldn't have provoked all this outcry. No grounds to go public. No, I'd have kept my mouth shut and started work on my next film, if it was nothing but a private dispute. But it was about something different. The reason we're going to court, with *Paris, Texas* 'on the screen at last' for a while now, is that what's at issue is not just the lying and cheating and skulduggery, and the selling down the river of a film and an independent producer, but an idea and a principle.

The cause is the 'auteur film' or whatever you want to call it, the phenomenon of the New German Cinema. For a decade now, this same New German Film has been the strongest argument in the world for a cinema that is not just a business but also an expressive form; something not only to do with money, but also, yes, with art. The idea of 'independent film-making' was as strongly held here as anywhere. And for a long time this idea had a home, created by the 'auteurs' themselves, in the institution of the Filmverlag der Autoren.

That this institution has become perverted into the very opposite, and has stopped looking after 'auteurs' and now exploits them or puts them out of business instead, that's the subject that's at issue, and that's what we're insisting on taking to court. The story of Filmverlag der Autoren and *Paris, Texas* shows that independent production in Germany will soon be at an end, if the distribution machinery actually acquires more power than the people who make the films and carry all the risks, and the responsibilities of producing them.

When such power is combined with cynicism and stupidity, things start to look really bleak.

It's to shed a bit of light on all this darkness that we're proceeding with the dispute, in court.

The dispute is as yet unresolved.

December 1984 – February 1985

An attempted description of an indescribable film*
From the first treatment for *Wings of Desire*

And we, spectators always, everywhere,
looking at, never out of, everything!

> Rilke, *8th Elegy* (tr. Leishman and Spender)

At first it's not possible to describe anything beyond a wish or a desire.

That's how it begins, making a film, writing a book, painting a picture, composing a tune, generally creating something.

You have a wish.

You wish that something might exist, and then you work on it until it does. You want to give something to the world, something truer, more beautiful, more painstaking, more serviceable, or simply something other than what already exists. And right at the start, simultaneous with the wish, you imagine what that 'something other' might be like, or at least you see something flash by. And then you set off in the direction of the flash, and you hope you don't lose your orientation, or forget or betray the wish you had at the beginning.

And in the end you have a picture or pictures of something, you have music, or something that operates in some new way, or a story, or this quite extraordinary combination of all these things: a film. Only with a film – as opposed to paintings, novels, music or inventions – you have to present an account of your desire; more, you even have to describe in advance the path you want to go with your film. No wonder, then, that so many films lose their first flash, their comet.

The thing I wished for and saw flashing was a film *in* and *about* Berlin.

A film that might convey something of the history of the city since 1945. A film that might succeed in capturing what I miss in so many films that are set here, something that seems to be so palpably there when you

*The German title of the film, *Der Himmel über Berlin*, translates literally as *The Sky over Berlin*.

arrive in Berlin: a feeling in the air and under your feet and in people's faces, that makes life in this city so different from life in other cities.

To explain and clarify my wish, I should add: it's the desire of someone who's been away from Germany for a long time, and who could only ever experience 'Germanness' in this one city. I should say I'm no Berliner. Who is nowadays? But for over twenty years now, visits to this city have given me my only genuine experiences of Germany, because the (hi)story that elsewhere in the country is suppressed or denied is physically and emotionally present here.

Of course I didn't want just to make a film about the place, Berlin. What I wanted to make was a film about people – people here in Berlin – that considered the one perennial question: how to live?

And so I have 'BERLIN' representing 'THE WORLD'.
I know of no place with a stronger claim.
Berlin is 'an historical site of truth'.
No other city is such a meaningful image,
such a PLACE OF SURVIVAL,
so exemplary of our century.
Berlin is divided like our world,
like our time,
like men and women,
young and old,
rich and poor,
like all our experience.
A lot of people say Berlin is 'crummy'.
I say: there is more reality in Berlin than any other city.
It's more a SITE than a CITY.
'To live in the city of undivided truth, to walk around with the invisible ghosts of the future and the past . . .'
That's my desire, on the way to becoming a film.

My story isn't about Berlin
because it's set there,
but because it couldn't be set anywhere else.
The name of the film will be:

THE SKY OVER BERLIN
because the sky is maybe the only thing
that unites these two cities,
apart from their past
of course. Will there be a common future?
'Heaven only knows.'
And language, much-invoked,
THE GERMAN LANGUAGE,
would seem to be shared also,
but in fact its plight
is the same as the city's:
one language comprises two
with a common past
but not necessarily a shared future.
And what of the present?
That's the subject of the film:
THE SKY OVER BERLIN.

OVER BERLIN?,
in, with, for, about Berlin . . .
What should such a film
'discuss', 'examine', 'depict', or 'touch on'?
And to what end?
As if every last particle
of Berlin hadn't been
tapped, taped, typed.
Not least because it's now 750 years old,
and has been promoted to LEGENDARY status,
which, while not unreasonable,
doesn't do anything to clarify
the condition 'Berlin',
rather the opposite.

THE SKY?,
the sky above it is the only
clear thing you can understand. The clouds

drift across it, it rains and snows and thunder-
and-lightnings, the moon sails through it
and sinks, the sun shines on the divided city,
today, as it did on the ruins in 1945
and the 'Front City' of the fifties,
as it did before there was any city here,
and as it will when there is no longer
any city.

Now what I want is starting to emerge:
namely to tell a story in Berlin.
(With the right stress, not for once
a STORY but:
A story.)
That requires objectivity, distance,
or, better yet, a vantage point. Because I don't want
to tell a STORY of UNITY, but
something harder:
ONE story about DIVISION.

Oh, Berlin isn't easy.
You're delighted to find moral
support on the back of the catalogue
for the exhibition LEGENDARY BERLIN
in this sentence from Heiner Müller:
'Berlin is the ultimate. Everything else is prehistory.
If history occurs, it will begin
in Berlin.'
Does that help?
In the film of course it's not HISTORY
but A story, though of course
a STORY may contain HISTORY,
images and traces of past history,
and intimations of what is to come. Anyway:
HEAVEN ONLY KNOWS!
You need the patience of an ANGEL

to sort all that out.
STOP!
It's right here at this point
that the film
DRIFTING
into my mind begins:
with ANGELS.
Yes, angels. A film with angels.
I know it's hard to grasp,
I myself can hardly grasp it yet:
'ANGELS'!

The genesis of the idea of having angels in my Berlin story is very hard to account for in retrospect. It was suggested by many sources at once. First and foremost, Rilke's *Duino Elegies*. Paul Klee's paintings too. Walter Benjamin's *Angel of History*. There was a song by the Cure that mentioned 'fallen angels', and I heard another song on the car radio that had the line 'talk to an angel' in it. One day, in the middle of Berlin, I suddenly became aware of that gleaming figure, 'the Angel of Peace', metamorphosed from being a warlike victory angel into a pacifist. There was an idea of four Allied pilots shot down over Berlin, an idea of juxtaposing and superimposing today's Berlin and the capital of the Reich, 'double images' in time and space; there have always been childhood images of angels as invisible, omnipresent observers; there was, so to speak, the old hunger for transcendence, and also a longing for the absolute opposite:
the longing for a comedy!
THE DEADLY EARNEST OF A COMEDY!

I'm amazed myself.
What's a film going to look like – what can it look like – possibly
a comedy – that has angels as its main characters?
With wings and with no flying??

I'm not after a 'screen-play' here. All I can do is go on describing what's 'ghosting around' in my imagination.

Inter alia, a WORKING METHOD for this film.

First I'll write down everything I want it to be, my ideas, images, stories and perhaps something like a rough structure, as well as a lot of research on Berlin, old newsreel footage and photographs. I've already begun on a street-by-street recce.

Then I'd like to shut myself away with the main actors and a writer for several weeks, and together mull over this material on 'angels' and 'Berlin', extend it, test it, adapt it or reject it, and finally come up with something we can all agree on, from which we can go on to make the film.

I spoke to Peter Handke about the project and he agreed to be involved, provided it was the kind of film you could pull out of your hat.

I agreed.

If my angel story is possible, then it is not as a calculated and sophisticated special-effects movie, but as an open affair, 'something pulled out of your hat'.

Particularly in Berlin, the city of conjurors.

If I were to give my story a prologue, it would go something like this:

WHEN GOD, ENDLESSLY DISAPPOINTED, FINALLY PREPARED TO TURN HIS BACK ON THE WORLD FOR EVER, IT HAPPENED THAT SOME OF HIS ANGELS DISAGREED WITH HIM AND TOOK THE SIDE OF MAN, SAYING HE DESERVED TO BE GIVEN ANOTHER CHANCE.

ANGRY AT BEING CROSSED, GOD BANISHED THEM TO WHAT WAS THEN THE MOST TERRIBLE PLACE ON EARTH: BERLIN.

AND THEN HE TURNED AWAY.

ALL THIS HAPPENED AT THE TIME THAT WE TODAY CALL: 'THE END OF THE SECOND WORLD WAR'.

SINCE THAT TIME, THESE FALLEN ANGELS FROM THE 'SECOND ANGELIC REBELLION' HAVE BEEN IMPRISONED IN THE CITY, WITH NO PROSPECT OF RELEASE, LET ALONE OF BEING READMITTED TO HEAVEN. THEY ARE CONDEMNED TO BE WITNESSES, FOR EVER NOTHING BUT ONLOOKERS, UNABLE TO AFFECT MEN IN THE SLIGHTEST, OR TO INTERVENE IN THE COURSE OF HISTORY. THEY ARE UNABLE TO SO MUCH AS MOVE A GRAIN OF SAND . . .

An introductory passage might go something like that. But there will be no introduction. All will gradually be brought out in the film, and make itself felt. The presence of the angels will explain itself.

(But that too is still at the stage of scheme and desire.)

After the prehistory, the story itself.

The angels have been in Berlin since the end of the war, condemned to remain there. They have no kind of power and are only onlookers, watching what happens without the slightest possibility of taking a hand in any of it. Previously, they had been able to influence things; as guardian angels they could at least give whispered counsel, but even that is now beyond them. Now they are just there, invisible to man, but themselves all-seeing.

They have been wandering around Berlin for forty years now. Each of them has his own 'patch' that he always walks, and 'his' people, of whom he has grown particularly fond and whose progress he follows with more attention than that of the other people he watches over. The angels don't only see everything, they hear everything too, even the most secret thoughts. They can sit next to the old woman on a bench in the Tiergarten and hear her thoughts, or stand behind the solitary train driver on the Underground and follow his thoughts. They have access to people in prison cells and hospital wards, and there is no business or political conference so secret that they aren't able to overhear it, nor any confessional, any psychiatrist's couch or any brothel. And if anyone lies, the angel can right away hear the difference between the thought and the spoken word.

People are unaware of their presence. Sometimes a child will catch a glimpse of an angel, and immediately forget it again. A grown-up can see them only in dreams, but on awakening he will forget them and dismiss them as a dream.

The years have gone by for our angels in Berlin, imperceptibly, in a recurring rhythm. They have seen almost two generations grow up and die, and soon it will be a third. They know every house and tree and shrub.

And more too:

They see beyond the world that manifests itself to people today. They can see it as it was when God turned away from it and they were banished, at the beginning of 1945. Behind the city of today, in its interstices or above it, as though frozen in time, are the ruins, the mounds of rubble, the burned chimneystacks and façades of the devastated city, only dimly visible sometimes, but always there in the background. There are other ghosts from the past too, shadowy presences visible to the angels: previously fallen angels and grim demons that had rampaged through the city and the country and put on their worst and bloodiest spectacle. These past figures are also hanging around Berlin; they too are unhoused and even more accursed. Admittedly, they have hardly any effect on the present, which apathetically lets them glide by. Unlike the angels, these spirits are indifferent to present-day life. They keep their own company in gloomy corners and past strongholds. Or they ride around in armoured personnel carriers, on motorbikes with sidecars, in tanks or black limos emblazoned with swastikas. When our angels appear, these figures run like rats. But there is hardly any contact or interaction, certainly no violent altercation between them and the angels.

Also dimly visible are the people of those times, queuing for food, on their way to the air-raid shelters, the 'women of the ruins' standing in long lines among the rubble, passing buckets from hand to hand, the abandoned children and the buses and trams of the time.

This latent past keeps appearing to the angels on their turns through present-day Berlin. If they want they can brush it away with a wave of the hand, but we know: incorporeal and timeless, this yesterday is still present everywhere, as a 'parallel world'.

Even though the angels have been watching and listening to people for such a long time, there are still many things they don't understand.

For example, they don't know and can't imagine what colours are. Or tastes and smells. They can guess what feelings are, but they can't experience them directly. As our angels are basically loving and good, they can't imagine things like fear, jealousy, envy or hatred. They are familiar with their expression, but not with the things themselves. They are naturally curious and would like to learn more, and from time to time they feel a pang of regret at missing out on all these things, not knowing what it's like throwing a stone, or what water or fire are like, or picking up some object in your hand, let alone touching or kissing a fellow human being.

All these things escape the angels. They are pure CONSCIOUSNESS, fuller and more comprehending than mankind, but also poorer. The physical and sensual world is reserved for human beings. It is the privilege of mortality, and death is its price.

So it can't come as a complete surprise that one day an angel has the extraordinary notion of giving up his angelic existence for a human life!

It's never been done. Perhaps the angels know as much. But the consequences are unknown.

The angel who had this astounding idea was falling in love with a woman, and it was his desire to be able to touch her that gave him the idea, with all its unpredictable consequences. He talks it over with his friends. To begin with they are shocked. But then they think about what it might entail, with the result that several of them agree to take the step together: to exchange their immortality for the brief flame of human life.

What persuades them is not the new experience they might have, or wanting to put an end to their troublesome impassivity, but the hope that something important might flow from their 'changing sides': the hope that by renouncing everlasting life, they might cause prodigious energies to be released which they hope to be able to collect and invest in one of their number, the most respected of them, an 'archangel', whom banishment reduced to the same level of powerlessness as all the others. He is the angel who lives in 'the Angel of Peace' and the great hope is that, by releasing this energy, he might become a real 'angel of peace', and help to bring peace to the world.

Anyway, the first (black-and-white) half of the film takes us to this point: a group of angels go over to human life and leave a transcendent, 'timeless' city for the actual Berlin of today.

One night, during a terrible storm, these new arrivals turn up in the city. Each in his own way, as befits his new human identity: one of them spins his car round a corner into a mercifully empty street, another finishes up on a roof, a third in a packed bar, others in a cinema, in the gutter, a bus, a backyard . . .

So now they are there, finally and irrevocably there. And it's in the second half of our story that the most extraordinary and thrilling things happen. For a start, everything is in colour. Not that it's 'more real' than previously. On the contrary. Perhaps the 'all-seeingness' of the angels was 'truer' than the colourful, three-rather-than-four-dimensional vision they have now. Anyway, their new type of seeing excites these recent earthlings. In fact, everything is thrilling, all these fresh sensations of the things they thought they were familiar with, but had never felt. Like Berlin itself.

As angels, they knew it better than any human did, but now they learn that it's all really completely different. Suddenly there are obstacles, distances, regulations and restrictions, among them the Wall itself, which has never previously been a barrier to them. That takes some getting used to.

But first come the 'sensations' of living. Breathing. Walking. Touching things. The first bite an apple, or perhaps a hot-dog at a corner stall. The first words addressed to a fellow human, and the first response. And finally, far into that first night: the first sleep. The bewilderment of dreams! And waking to the reality of the following morning.

All these 'feelings'!

They assail our adventurers like viruses attacking a man with no immunity.

There is fear, previously unknown to them. Nothing in their angelic existence had prepared them for it. In eternity there was no fear, now in this death-shadowed world it's there. Several of the angels despair at it, one in fact almost goes mad, and another soon takes his own new life. But most adapt. Especially when they remember there was one human faculty which, as angels, they had had a particular admiration for: a sense of humour. 'You've just got to laugh': now they understand why, and they feel liberated by it. They realized earlier that it does no good to a man to take everything seriously.

All in all, they still know a lot of what they knew as angels. And they know about all the other spirits around them – though they are no longer visible. They know their old friends are there, and they know they are continually being watched and 'shadowed'. They walk their old 'beats', insofar as they are still accessible to them. And they talk to the angels, knowing they are there and merely unable to reply. They tell them about their new experiences, both joyful and painful. Because of their conversations with angels, they are looked at askance by their new fellow humans.

I hope that won't befall the author of this 'story with angels'.

1986

For (not about) Ingmar Bergman

It seems to me presumptuous to try to write or say anything about Ingmar Bergman, and any account is an impertinence: these films stand alone like great beacons in film history. There is nothing one would welcome so much as their liberation from all commentaries, all the ballast of the history of their interpretation; let them shine out once more! It seems to me that there is no other contemporary director whose work is so frequently filtered through the murky windows of 'opinion'; there are no other films as deserving of simply being seen without being pre-analysed as those of Ingmar Bergman. I want to take this opportunity of sending him my best wishes on his birthday – and of not boring him with another 'opinion'. I'd also like to promise him – and myself – that I will go and see all his films again, and this time without the burden of the history of my own responses to them.

When I recollect these, I see myself as a schoolboy sneaking out to the cinema with my girlfriend (although forbidden or, in fact, *because* forbidden by school, church and parents) to see *The Silence*. I see myself coming out of it deeply affected, and avoiding all discussion of it with my schoolfriends on subsequent days, just because in our discussions I couldn't have expressed its effect on me. I see myself a couple of years later, as a medical student, stumbling out of a late double bill of *The Seventh Seal* and *Wild Strawberries*, and then spending the rest of the night walking in the rain, bewildered and agitated by all these questions of life and death. And then I see myself another couple of years on, a film student now, rejecting *Persona* and all Bergman's work, arguing instead for a cinema without psychology, where everything should be visible 'on the surface of things'. I think with some embarrassment of my rather glib speeches against the 'depth' and 'portentousness' of Bergman's films, as opposed to the 'physical quality' of the American cinema. And, after another interval I see myself, by now a film-maker myself and in

America, emerging from a cinema in San Francisco having cried buckets at a screening of *Cries and Whispers*, a film that made the 'European cinema of *Angst* and introversion' that I'd despised ten years ago look like a long-lost home to me, somewhere I would be far happier in than here, in the 'promised land' of the cinema where I was now, and where the 'surface' that I'd once so admired had in the meantime become so smooth and hard that there was really nothing 'behind' it any more. And if as a student I'd inveighed against that 'deep' cinema, I now discovered in myself a longing for 'depth', and felt more than reconciled to Ingmar Bergman.

I'm no expert; I see films the same way as everyone else does: as part of an audience. I know that seeing a film is a 'subjective' process – i.e. you only see the film which the 'objective film' up there on the screen projects on to your inner eye. I think that's even truer of Ingman Bergman's films: we see 'ourselves' in them, but not 'as in a mirror', no, better than that, 'as in a film' ABOUT US.

July 1988

A history of imaginary films
Letter to the editors of *Cahiers du Cinéma*

Dear Alain Bergala and Serge Toubiana,

My thanks to you. It is by turns an honour, a responsibility and a joy to be the editor of this fortieth edition of the *Cahiers*. This number will be out late, I can just tell it will. As with everything I write, it will be late and miss its deadline. It's the only way I've ever written. Writing is fear: a script, an article, a letter, it's always the same, the words are inevitably late; it seems to be in their nature.

The paradoxical thing is that films begin with words, and that words determine whether the images are allowed to be born. The words are like the headland that a film has to steer round to reach the image. It's at that point that many films go under. For all sorts of reasons (of which lack of money is the worst), they remain locked up in scripts that are never shot. Looked at like that, film history is like an iceberg: you only ever see the 10 per cent or so of completed films, the liberated image; the majority of them remain imprisoned in the ice, forever below the surface. My first idea was to devote this issue to these 'underwater' films. We sent out letters to friends and cinéastes, asking them to let us see the first pages of the script of some film of theirs that was never made. In the case of deceased directors, we searched for such scripts ourselves. It could be the beginning of a history of imaginary films, parallel to the history of all lost films.

But happily there were many directors who had no 'aborted' projects and no abandoned scripts in their desk drawers. So we extended our idea of the imaginary film to include the 'roots', the sources of films. A few directors have sent in replies along those lines. For my own part, I've tried to recall the origins of my own films.

At what exact moment is a film born? Or perhaps it would be better to say conceived? That's an apt expression: it always seemed to me that my films were created out of the meeting of two ideas or two complementary images. Their roots seem to belong to one of two great families: 'images' (experiences, dreams, imagination) and 'stories' (myths, novels, miscellaneous news items). Antonioni's wonderful book *Nothing But Lies* describes the moment when the film-maker's lying in wait for whatever it is that sparks off the desire for a film:

> I don't know anything about the way a film is born, nothing about the manner of it, the lying-in, the 'big bang', the first three minutes. Whether the images in those first three minutes are born out of their author's deep desire, or if – in an ontological sense – they merely are what they are. I wake up one morning with my head full of images. I don't know where they come from, or how or why. They recur in the following days and months; I can't do anything about them, and I do nothing to drive them away. I'm happy to contemplate them and I make notes in my mind, which I write down in a book some time.

After the story of films that went astray and were never made, one could go on to the still more compendious story of those films that never even made scripts: suppressed ideas and images, dreams that no one wrote down on awakening, miscellaneous news clippings left and lost in the drawer, beginnings of stories one witnessed with one's own eyes and then forgot all about.

As a boy, I often used to ask myself if there really was a God who saw everything. And how he managed not to forget any of it: the motion of the clouds in the sky, every individual's gestures and footsteps, the dreams . . . I said to myself that while it was impossible to imagine such a memory existing, it was even sadder and more desolating to think that it didn't and that everything was forgotten. This childish panic still upsets me. The story of all phenomena would be infinitely great, the story of all surviving images infinitesimally small.

For centuries only poets and painters have taken up this gigantic work of memory. Then photographers made a valuable contribution, then cinema people, with ever greater sums of money and ever less understanding. Nowadays it's mostly television that conserves images. But the inflation of electronic images offered us by television seems so unworthy of being recalled that you have to ask yourself whether it wouldn't be better to return to the old traditions of poets and painters. It's better to have a few images that are full of life than masses of meaningless ones.

It's the vision that determines whether anything has been seen or not.

I'd like to thank all the friends and film-makers who contributed to this issue. They have the vision of painters and poets. I would urge you not to concentrate on the piteous documents of films that were never made, but rather to view the short history of the films that do exist with joy and with gratitude, and to be daily more astonished at the great imaginary history that envelops us all.

Editorial for the 400th issue of Cahiers du Cinéma, *guest-edited by W. W.*

Le Souffle de l'Ange

Music First

'My life was saved by Rock and Roll'   Velvet Underground

When I first began making films – shorts – my starting-point was music. *Alabama*, for instance, came out of the Dylan song 'All Along the Watchtower', which is sung twice in the film, first in Dylan's version, then in Jimi Hendrix's. In between, like an insert, was the story. The first time I worked with Peter Handke was on the short *Three American LPs*. There was also another music idea I had that involved showing just the group red leader on the screen.

I was much more involved with music than film at the time. I can remember loads of record sleeves; the ones I liked best were the ones that featured pictures of the groups, standing together in some arrangement. I liked Van Morrison and Them very much, and the Animals and the Pretty Things. What was on the covers, with the Kinks for instance, corresponded to my idea of cinema: filming people head on, with a fixed camera, and keeping a certain distance. I made my best musical discoveries by going by the sleeves.

We made a film about the English group Ten Years After; I did the camerawork and a friend, Mathias Weiss, was responsible for the production. The film consists of one single shot that goes on for about twenty minutes, and the soundtrack is the group's version of the old Willie Dixon number, 'Spoonful'. We wanted to film it in Cinemascope, but we couldn't afford it, so we invented 16 mm Cinemascope. Two black masking-strips in front of the camera made it look like Cinemascope. We drove up from Munich with the film school's camera to see the group in London. Our dream was to put music on the screen, preferably without any cutting at all.

My first full-length film, *Summer in the City*, came out of the same desire to put my then Top Ten on the screen. Hence a storyline that would allow us to use lots of songs and have jukeboxes, car radios or tape-recorders in all the scenes. We had the Kinks, the Troggs, Lovin' Spoonful and Chuck Berry. The trouble was, I hadn't got the rights to any of the songs, so the film could never be screened. *Summer in the City* was in the same vein as the shorts, but for the first time I had a small budget at my disposal. We used everything we shot; we hardly ever did more than one take on anything: a two-and-a-half hour film was made with a fifteen-minute budget. That way I could get in a lot of music. The characters listened to records and told each other short, fragmented stories. At the end Hanns Zischler calls the cinema information service and repeats all the titles in a loud voice. It goes on for ages, and it's my favourite scene in the whole film.

Filmkritik

From 1967 to 1970 I studied at the Munich Film School. They were revolutionary times. We threw out our teachers and devised our own courses. We were the first year's intake at the school, which made us indispensable. Without us, there would be no school. During this time I worked for the magazine *Filmkritik*; I liked the people very much: Frieda Grafe, Enno Patalas, Helmut Färber and Herbert Linder. It was at this time that I started thinking seriously about the cinema. I thought I might write about films professionally, as a film historian. It seemed most unlikely that I would ever make films myself.

My first review was a rather chance affair, after I saw *Wavelength* by Michael Snow at Knocke. The film didn't have many supporters, most of the audience walked out, and I wrote an article to defend it. I submitted it to the magazine *Film*; Peter Handke did work for them and I asked him to try to get it accepted. That encouraged me to go on; I didn't see myself as a director at all.

Filmverlag

The mere fact of its existence made the Filmverlag der Autoren the epicentre of the entire German cinema. The Filmverlag brought together fifteen or so film-makers, almost all of them beginners belonging to the same generation: Uwe Brandner, who made a very good film, *I Love You, I'll Kill You*; Thomas Schamoni who had made his first film, *A Big Grey-Blue Bird*; Peter Lilienthal, Hark Bohm ... Other partners in the company were screenwriters like Veith von Fürstenberg, who co-wrote *Alice in the Cities* with me and only made his own first feature-length film much later. The essential thing was the existence of an autonomous production structure. Maybe the company didn't produce much significant work to begin with. We realized later that it wasn't enough just to be independent producers. Gradually the company concentrated on its distribution side; that's when Fassbinder and Herzog joined us.

The German film industry at that time was absolutely atrocious. It made Karl May films, so-called 'Heimatfilme' and stacks of soft porn, all of it kitsch and only for home consumption. They were contemptuous of us, called us beginners, '*Jungfilmer*' – from those people it was a put-down. Unlike the *Nouvelle Vague*, we never thought or hoped or meant to 'improve' the industry, to join it, or even to replace it: we saw our activity as an alternative to it. No models, no tradition, no one whose place we wanted to usurp. The Filmverlag was a kind of co-operative for us. There was unusual solidarity among us – the only capital we had. There was another group based up in Hamburg where people like Werner Nekes and Klaus Wyborny founded a co-operative that distributed my own first short films. But they stayed with non-narrative films, whereas our own movement in Munich was that of the 'School of Sensibility' – another derogatory label. For all that, and again unlike the *Nouvelle Vague*, we never had discussions about aesthetics; we never tried for a group style.

The Goalkeeper's Fear of the Penalty

This film derives from my friendship with Peter Handke. I read the novel before publication, and I told Handke: 'Reading it gives me the impression of a film, it's like the description of a film.' He replied in a slightly joky way: 'Well then, why don't you make it!' I'd never written a script in my life, didn't even know what one looked like. I took the book and divided it up into scenes; there wasn't a lot to do – its structure was like a film's already. It was very simple, every sentence translated into a shot.

Peter Przygodda, who'd helped on the editing of *Summer in the City*, told me about a wonderful actor called Arthur Brauss. My own idea had been to have a real goalkeeper in the part: I thought of Wolfgang Fahrian, who played in the national side for a while. He played for Cologne FC, and I worshipped him as a kid; he was a great keeper. I met him to talk about it, but it was never really on, filming during the week, between match days. I didn't know any actors, and so I met Arthur Brauss. What really impressed me about him was that he'd worked as a cowboy in Texas, which wasn't bad going for a German actor. In this small town in Texas he'd joined an amateur theatre group and done Shakespeare plays. Then Brauss became an actor, and appeared mostly in action films, usually as a cowboy in spaghetti-Westerns, one of the twenty baddies. Kai Fischer, another boyhood idol of mine, played the hotel manageress. She was in a lot of fifties films, playing wild girls, awful parts, but I liked her. And then there was Libgart Schwarz, Peter Handke's wife, who'd appeared in *Summer in the City*, where she was the only professional actor. She's wonderful in *The Goalkeeper*.

There's one shot in the film that I particularly liked when I saw it again: a close-up of an apple on a tree. It's a complete mystery, nothing to do with the story. Early on in the film, I wanted to cut in a shot of an object; but while we loaded the second camera the light changed, so we couldn't shoot it. As a result, I decided with the cameraman Robby Müller to keep the second camera always loaded and ready, to shoot inserts like that. By the end, mostly on days off, we had about thirty shots, none of them anything to do with the story. We called that roll of film our 'art cassette'; like my idea of the 'imaginary film', this was a kind of parallel film, a film of objects, no story, and that strange and beautiful apple is the only thing that survived from it. We slotted it in at the last minute before doing the mix, and I'm glad now that Peter Przygodda forced me to put it in.

The Goalkeeper owes a lot to Hitchcock, more than any of my other films. Hitchcock was an inspiration behind Handke's book too. For the shot where Bloch wakes up and sees his jacket hanging on a chair, I used the same technique as Hitchcock in the famous tower shot in *Vertigo*: the camera rolls forward and simultaneously zooms backwards. As for the old lady who watches Bloch in the bus, she's straight out of *The Lady Vanishes*.

When I wrote the script, I again had a whole series of songs I wanted to put into the film. Five or six finally made it, including – in my favourite scene, the sequence where Bloch takes the bus out into the countryside – 'The Lion Sleeps Tonight' by the Tokens. It was the first time Robby and I had gone out across country, from Vienna to the Yugoslav border. Our first bit of road-movie – we were terribly proud of it. Then suddenly I was able to make a film with proper money, in 35 mm. It was completely unexpected. My delight was put in question by the film that resulted.

The Scarlet Letter

The television people who had co-produced *The Goalkeeper*, Westdeutscher Rundfunk, were very pleased with it. Although I was naïvely proud of my work, it didn't occur to me that I might become a professional film-maker. My real profession was writing, or maybe painting. I was surprised to be offered a new film; they had a project and were looking for a director for it. There was no way I could turn it down: a chance to make another film!

I liked Hawthorne's novel, which I'd read when I was fifteen or sixteen. It might have been the first book I read in English. There was a great cast: Senta Berger, who was a star in Germany; she'd made films in the States, and she was very big in Italy. There was Lou Castel, who'd just been deprived of his Italian citizenship and went through the filming in a state of somnambulism. The Puritans were played by Spaniards, the Indian by a former *torero* whose legs had been gored.

It was a disaster. I very quickly felt I'd walked into a trap. I should have stopped filming and got out, but the financial viability of the distributor depended on my completing it.

Alice in the Cities

The filming of *The Scarlet Letter* was hellish, but there was one short scene between Rüdiger Vogler and little Yella Rottländer, a very precious moment, when I said to myself that if the film was all like this it would be bliss. During the editing, I listened to Chuck Berry's song 'Memphis'. For most of the song the words give you the impression it's about a woman, but just at the end you're told he's talking about a six-year-old girl. I said to myself: that scene with Rüdiger and little Yella, with this song over it, would make a film. Near the end of *Alice in the Cities* you see Philip Winter at a Chuck Berry concert and he's singing 'Memphis'. Another starting-point: while I was travelling in America I'd taken a lot of old-style Polaroid pictures, the type where it takes a minute or so and then the fully developed photograph comes out. We'd heard rumours of an amazing piece of equipment that took pictures and you could actually see the pictures as they developed. We wrote off to Polaroid and they lent us a couple of these new cameras long before they appeared on the market. I've still got the first picture I took with one in a café in New York City.

I'd written the story – but not the script – and a friend asked me along to the press night of *Paper Moon*; I'd loved Peter Bogdanovich's *The Last Picture Show*. It was a disaster for me: the story I'd written was exactly like *Paper Moon* – a man travelling around with a little girl, and returning her to his aunt at the end. Just like in my film. Plus Tatum O'Neal looked just like my Alice – only Rüdiger Vogler wasn't exactly a Ryan O'Neal. I was appalled and wanted to chuck it in. I called my production chief to cancel the project. In that desperate state I went to Los Angeles for a screening of my first three films. I remember the showing of *Summer in the City*: there was no one in the cinema except the projectionist and me and we both stayed to the end.

I'd met Sam Fuller in Germany while he was filming *Dead Pigeon on Beethovenstrasse*. As I was in town, I gave him a ring. He asked me round to breakfast with him at 10 a.m. We ended up sitting at the table till night: plenty of vodka, wonderful Polish-Jewish cuisine, and I ended up telling him the story of my film, and how, because of Bogdanovich, I wasn't able to make it any more. He said something like that had once happened to him too. He'd seen *Paper Moon* and asked me to tell him what happened in my film. I began, but he was too impatient to hear me out: 'OK, OK, I see the problem.' And then he started telling me my plot as he saw it. It sounded nothing like *Paper Moon*, and it wasn't exactly what I had written either, but suddenly the film seemed possible again.

That night I called Germany and said we were going ahead.

With *Alice in the Cities* I found my individual voice in the cinema. Much later I realized that all those years there had been a kind of pendulum motion between two poles in my work: films on personal themes in black and white, and colour films adapted from literary works: *Summer in the City* and *The Goalkeeper*, *Alice in the Cities* and *False Movement*, *Kings of the Road* and *The American Friend*. (I leave *The Scarlet Letter* out of this scheme altogether.)

False Movement

I had no further projects planned. But since the time of *The Goalkeeper*, Peter Handke and I had talked vaguely about Goethe's *Wilhelm Meister's Apprenticeship*, and a possible collaboration on it. One day Peter bent my ear on the telephone; he felt like taking up that idea. We both adored Goethe's book, but felt that its emancipatory movement couldn't get you anywhere today. Travel as apprenticeship, as something towards understanding the world, that wasn't an idyll we could seriously share. So our film would be the journey of someone hoping to understand the world, but actually the opposite would happen: he would realize that his movement had taken him to a dead end; effectively he wouldn't have moved an inch. Hence the title: *False Movement*.

I was just then doing some bread-and-butter television work (*From the Crocodile Family*), so Peter wrote the screenplay. It was practically without directorial notes and didn't even specify locations. Handke's text left me a lot of freedom, and in fact I didn't change a word of his dialogue. After the filming was over, when we were looking at the film together during editing, we added a voiceover that hadn't originally been planned.

What sparked off the film was Peter, our shared pleasure in Goethe, and my urge to go out and discover the German landscape. In the middle of the film, approaching the Rhine, that long climb, you see in the distance the small town of Boppard where my mother was born and where I spent a great part of my childhood, immediately after the war. I've always remembered the great River Rhine, but in a vague, occluded way, so to speak. I was desperate to go there, but Peter favoured a flat landscape. I also wanted to travel right across Germany, start at the northernmost point and go all the way to the southernmost. Early on, I looked at a map of Germany for a place in the north, and there was a little town I chose purely for the sake of its name: Glückstadt.* And the film was to end at Germany's highest point, the Zugspitze. A lot of my films were inspired by poring over maps.

For this film we needed a girl of thirteen or so: Mignon, as Goethe calls her. I've never done regular casting and I hate it, so I looked around in discotheques for a bit. I was out with Lisa Kreuzer when we saw her. She was beautiful, and she had something else too: in her eyes, in her feline movements. We heard her friends calling her 'Stassi'.

Lisa went up to her and said we would like to speak to her parents. The next day we saw her mother and learned that the girl was Nastassia, the daughter of Klaus Kinski. She celebrated her fourteenth birthday during the filming. She'd never stood in front of a camera before, and she would often get giggling fits in the middle of a scene. She was wonderful, though, still a child, but with something incredibly touching about her. Half the crew were in love with her. It was clear from the first rushes that she was a born actress, even though she hadn't given it any thought herself. We noticed what presence she had and made her part bigger.

Hanna Schygulla I'd known before she'd appeared in films. I used to go to the same bar as Fassbinder, the 'Bungalow', where she would often be dancing in front of the jukebox. That's where he first saw her too. When we made *False Movement* she'd already been in about a dozen of his films. She was always very lively in Fassbinder's films, and visibly less so in mine. I was rather upset by that.

Kings of the Road

The inspiration for this film was a photo-reportage: during the Depression, Walker Evans travelled the American South on an assignment from the Farm Security Administration. The series of photographs he took are absolutely distinctive, and go right to the heart of the Depression. The part of Germany we drove through, the no-man's-land by the East

*Bliss.

German frontier, struck me as depressed too – everyone was leaving, it was an area without hope. We felt we were producing a kind of report, a little in the manner of Walker Evans.

You can detect the presence of Walker Evans, for instance in the scene where Bruno and Robert find these barracks; partly also, I suppose, because they were built by American GIs and have American graffiti on them. We found that little bit of America in no-man's-land in Germany; it's as if our muse and the physical reality coincided there. Often what we saw was determined by Evans's photographs. We would sometimes pull up on the road to shoot scenes because something in the landscape or the building happened to grab us. Once, we passed an old caravan that was being used as a mobile caff, or rather I noticed it and about a mile later I said: 'Robby, did you see what I saw?' and he said: 'Yes, and I was amazed you didn't want to stop for it.' So we turned round, followed by the cavalcade of the crew, and we spent the rest of the day filming in and around that caff. We'd never have noticed it, if it hadn't been for Walker Evans's photographs. The same applies to the crumbling old factory. We stopped because it was made of corrugated iron. When we were looking at Walker Evans's photos, we thought how lucky he was because all the houses in them are corrugated iron which comes out beautifully in black and white.

In the end you realize that you're directed by what you've already seen; if it hadn't been for that, you'd be lost in the superabundance of every-thing there is to see.

Our first recce was to track down all the cinemas along the German–German border. It turned out that half of the cinemas listed in the phonebook had since closed down.

We usually didn't book hotel rooms ahead, although there were twelve to fifteen of us. So from time to time some would have to sleep in the truck. Our shooting schedule wasn't fixed in advance either: we were totally free. In the middle of the filming we decided, just like that, to leave the border area and go and film on an island on the Rhine; that meant a detour of 500 kilometres. It was the first time I was unfettered, and my own producer. To begin with, I worked on the script the night before with the two lead actors, Rüdiger Vogler and Hanns Zischler. But quite soon they asked me to carry on alone: they preferred seeing their scenes in the morning, just before shooting them. I remember we had to stop filming once for two days, just at the time we came across those American barracks. Up until then the cinemas along the frontier had been our fixed points. But for a while now we'd felt the need for a big scene, a kind of showdown between the two main characters; and everyone agreed that these barracks should be the place where they break their long silence, speak their minds, and split. It took me two days to write the scene – and the crew were waiting. It was the hardest writing I've ever had to do. There were so many important things to be said in the scene, about the way the Americans have colonized our subconscious, about the loneliness between men and women. In the morning, when I showed the actors what I'd written, they said it was too explicit, too much on the surface. But we failed to reach a deeper level, so we kept it. That night I swore I'd never get in such a panic again, and that there'd darn well be a script next time.

The American Friend

On this film, our model wasn't a photographer but the painter Edward Hopper. But more important was my desire to work with a book by Patricia Highsmith. Peter Handke had mentioned me to her, we exchanged letters and finally we met. First of all I asked after *The Cry of the Owl*, then *The Tremor of Forgery*, then two other novels, but in each case the rights were unavailable. Finally she felt sorry for me and gave me the manuscript she was working on at the time, *Ripley's Game*. The story is set in France and Germany: the main character lives outside Paris and commits his murders in Hamburg. In the film we changed that around, and that turned out to be a much more significant change than I'd naïvely thought.

From the outset I had a pretty clear idea of Ripley – especially once I was certain that Dennis Hopper would be playing him – but it was harder to get a line on Jonathan, who seemed to me to be purely a victim. I started to move in on his character. I could have him do roughly what I do myself: frame pictures. He could restore gadgets and objects from the early days of the cinema; that way, I could imagine his life in some detail. The flat he lives in with his family: the lampshade with the moving train on it in the nursery, the zoetrope next to the telephone in the hall. The shop where he works: a stereoscope from the turn of the century, a moving image of a face that smiles the first time he meets Ripley. To reinforce his identification with myself, I made Jonathan sing two of my favourite songs to himself. While he's sweeping up in his shop, he sings 'There is too much on my mind and there is nothing I can do about it' by the Kinks. And at the end, in Ripley's car, he sings 'Baby, you can drive my car' by the Beatles.

Since I had trouble putting a face on the numerous gangsters in the book, I had the idea of having them all played by film-director friends of mine: Sam Fuller, Daniel Schmidt, Gérard Blain, Peter Lilienthal, Jean Eustache and finally Nicholas Ray. I didn't originally envisage Nick's part in the film. In the novel there is the painter Derwatt who paints forgeries. We were in New York to film scenes for the subplot on porn films made there and distributed in Europe. Sam Fuller was down to play the Mafia man who finances the porn films. But Sam didn't show up – he was doing a recce in Yugoslavia. We were all hanging around, the entire crew not knowing if and when he would come.

While we were all waiting, Pierre Cottrell introduced me to Nicholas Ray. He'd had to go to court over some rent affair; after the hearing we had supper together. Then we sat up all night playing backgammon. The next day we saw him again, and I told him I was in trouble because of Sam. Nick said: 'You're in a pickle. You could spend your life waiting. Much better to rewrite your script!' So I cut out the whole Mafia story and put in the painter instead. Nick was delighted with the suggestion that he play the painter; we wrote his scenes together very quickly, in a single night. That's how we managed to have scenes between Dennis Hopper and Nick – the two hadn't seen each other since *Rebel Without a Cause*. On the last day of filming, when we'd stopped thinking about him, Sam turned up. We shot one more scene, the only one in the film that had the Mafia in it.

Hammett

Hammett was a commission. I was in Australia, where I was working on a science-fiction story – this was Christmas 1977 – when I got a telegram from Coppola asking me if I'd like to make a film about Dashiell Hammett, based on Joe Gores's novel.

I had three books with me, and one of them was *Red Harvest*, my favourite Hammett. Later, when we started on our preparations, I hoped to be able to incorporate a bit of *Red Harvest* in the film. That would have allowed me to film in Butte, Montana. (In the novel, the name of the town is Poisonville, but Hammett said in interviews that Poisonville was based on Butte.) I'd been there. The inhabitants were gradually burning the place down to collect on the insurance. Already economically dead, the town was in the process of disappearing off the face of the earth. The atmosphere there was strangely like the twenties, as Hammett describes it: an air of corruption and desperation. Unfortunately, we weren't able to get the rights to *Red Harvest* because an Italian producer was holding them for Bertolucci, who'd been working on the project for a very long time.

I put an immense amount of almost schoolish work into *Red Harvest*. Hammett originally wrote it for the magazine *Black Mask*, where it appeared in instalments. Three or four years later he revised it for book publication. I compared the two versions, line by line. When I finished, I understood how Hammett wrote. The two versions are so strikingly different, it was as though Hammett had jumped from the first treatment of the story straight to the final edit.

I wanted to show someone who had been a detective, and who starts writing during an illness; how he acquires a style and becomes a writer through describing a line of work he knows from personal experience, and turns it into literature. An astonishing career. Francis Coppola more or less shared my ideas, but he was producing it for Orion Pictures and they were expecting an action film. When Francis saw the rough cut, the film was even more centred on the writer, and he was afraid the studio might reject it outright.

It's possible to ruin a film by over-preparation. That's why, years later, I started on *Wings of Desire* when nothing had been properly sorted out. I sort of felt that 'another two weeks and we'll be really well prepared, but the film will have gone to seed'. That was the problem with *Hammett*. For instance, there was a radio version that was scripted by Tom Pope, the second writer we took on after Joe Gores. One day Francis said he didn't want to read any more scripts, so we had this idea of doing a radio show: he gave me a sound-man, I had a free hand to pick actors, make noises, add the music, mix, whatever. It was nice work. Sam Shepard played Hammett and Gene Hackman played Jimmy Ryan. The version lasted two hours. Then Francis suggested commissioning a sketch-artist to make drawings of all the shots: put them on video, accompanied by the radio-track, and he would be able to 'see' the whole film, sound and pictures. Then he wanted to feed the video sketch into a computer. Each time we had a scene filmed and edited, it would replace a bit of the sketch. But by the time we actually saw the video, we were completely fed up with the film. Francis threw the script out the window and said we should start again from scratch. Tom Pope replied by wanting to throw the computer out instead: three of us had to hold him down . . . But, to get back to Coppola's dream of 'seeing' a film before it's been shot: it turns the eventual film into the mere execution of something that already exists, into a kind of *déjà vu*. That's why 90 per cent of American films are failures, and it taught me that the preparations mustn't be overdone, the story mustn't be formulated in advance too much, before it goes down on film.

In the event I made two *Hammett*s. First I filmed and edited a version by Dennis O'Flaherty – he was the third scriptwriter we used. There was only the ending still to do, less than ten minutes. And then Francis said once more: we'll start again, hire a new scriptwriter and he can use some of the existing scenes. And that's what happened. The next writer, Ross Thomas, retained about four or five scenes and rewrote everything else. I reshot the film in just four weeks. In the final edit, we used about 30 per cent of the original version and 70 per cent of the new one.

The one thing that survived all these adventures was Coppola's endeavour to let me make a film. We were both bloody-minded enough to see it through.

Nick's Film/Lightning over Water

While O'Flaherty was working on the third version of the *Hammett* script, I had a couple of months off. I called Nicholas Ray in New York. Nick had cancer and had just been operated on for the third time; he'd been out of hospital for a few weeks, but was still getting radiotherapy. I used to call on him whenever I was passing through New York. He once said to me: 'If I only could work a bit, even if it was a film with a tiny budget.' I had a few weeks' time now, and Nick said straight out: 'Come to New York so we can make a film together.'

It wasn't possible to do anything with the scripts he had ready: they would have involved too much preparation. So he started writing a treatment based on the character he'd played in *The American Friend*. A painter, sick with cancer, has a Chinese friend who runs a launderette downstairs from his apartment. He begins producing 'fakes' of his own paintings, which are hanging in a gallery. He then breaks into the gallery, substitutes the fakes for his originals, buys a junk with the money he gets for them and sets off with his friend to China. There's an American expression 'to take a slow boat to China', meaning 'to die'. That was Nick's idea. In the film you see us talking about it: mightn't it be better, instead of being a painter who breaks into a gallery, to have him be a film director who tries to get into a lab to steal the negative of his film? (And in actual fact, Nick's film *We Can't Go Home Again* was locked up in a New York lab and no longer belonged to him.) When I suggested to Nick that he play himself, he replied: fine, but on condition that you appear in the film as well. 'You have to expose yourself, too.'

That was how the film began: I arrive at his house, and we talk about the film we're going to make together. After that it got complicated. Nick would often get behind the camera; for a few days he directed, thereafter he lacked the strength. He was going into hospital every day and by the end he was staying there overnight. I was in constant contact with his doctors. They assured me it was better for him to be making the film than to be plunged into depression. We carried on to the end, we even filmed in the hospital with a video camera, then in his loft once more, a scene between Tom Farrell and me, when Nick was already dead.

I'd never been in a film. We improvised the first scenes, recorded the dialogue on tape, and played them back and corrected them. That was how the script developed. Nick held my hand. We would shoot a scene five or six times and I felt very ill at ease: with each take, my performance grew stiffer and more artificial. Nick helped me to keep a sense of what the scene was about, even at the end of several takes. He was terribly amused by my struggles as an actor, and I'd have been lost without his help. I would turn to him and ask, how do actors do that? And he would know, he'd taught at the Actors' Studio for years . . .

The State of Things

In order to explain how this film came about, I have to start with a project that never came off: *Stiller*, after Max Frisch's novel. It was during that period of uncertainty between the first and second *Hammett*. Francis Coppola was making *One From the Heart* with Fred Forrest. I was in Zurich, to get the feel of Stiller's terrain, and I started writing. I'd met Frisch in New York, and got together with Bruno Ganz, the only possible actor for the part. That was in the winter of 1980. But it didn't work. For a start, I didn't feel comfortable in Zurich, and then there were problems with an American woman who had the rights to the book. She wanted a say in the casting, so I said forget it.

Isabelle Weingarten, who was shooting *Le Territoire* in Portugal with Raoul Ruiz, told me about the money troubles they were having: they had run out of stock and there was a chance the filming would have to be suspended. It happened that we had a few rolls in a fridge in Berlin, and so, instead of flying straight back to New York as intended, I set off for Lisbon to see Isabelle and give Raoul the film. What should I find but a calmly working crew. No running around, no frayed nerves. It was idyllic. We had 200 technicians working on *Hammett* and problems with everything: the script, studio supervision, etc. – and here in the forests of Sintra they were working calmly and easily, under no pressure. Only they didn't have any money. It was like a lost paradise for me. I stayed on, I went for walks, and on one of them I saw this deserted hotel that had been wrecked by a storm or hurricane the winter before. It looked like a beached whale.

I said to myself: you've got everything you need to make a film here. The ocean, a fantastic location, the most westerly point in Europe – the nearest point to America. I wanted to make something that reflected my own position between the continents and my fear of making a film in America. I asked Henri Alekan and Raoul's crew and actors if they'd be prepared to stay on and make another film the moment *Le Territoire* was finished. They all said of course; no one really took me seriously. I went to New York to ask Chris Sievernich to try to rustle up some financial backing. We began filming a month later.

Perhaps I made a mistake in breaking off the film-within-a-film. It was a science-fiction story that we were shooting with Henri in day for night. This prologue was supposed to take just two days, but there wasn't enough sun and so it went on and on. After a week of it – the film-within-a-film was called *The Survivors* – the actors were really enjoying themselves in their parts and their costumes, and basically everyone was terribly keen just to carry on: a B-movie based on Allan Dwan's picture *The Most Dangerous Man Alive*. We'd all gone to Sintra to see that together, and the atmosphere of Dwan's film coloured the whole of *The State of Things*, not just the prologue.

I had misgivings about the pan shot that moves from the science-fiction film to the story of its production. It was like an abortion. We sacrificed the story for a film that says it's impossible to have a story in a film. It wasn't until the end of this '*film à thèse*', the American episode, that another little bit of fiction rescued this anti-fiction film. Allan Dwan won out in the end.

Paris, Texas

I met Sam Shepard during the *Hammett* saga. He, incidentally, would have been my ideal Hammett, and for two years I tried to persuade them to let me have him. I didn't succeed, and in the end it was him who said: Look, you've got enough trouble with the film as it is without trying to get me into it. While I was filming the second version of *Hammett* in the Zoetrope studios, Sam and Jessica Lange were shooting *Frances* next door. He showed me some of his writing, poems and short stories; the manuscript was called *Transfiction*, and later became *Motel Chronicles*.

Somehow we lost contact. I finished *Hammett* and spent a year writing a screenplay based on Peter Handke's *Slow Homecoming* and his play *The Long Way Round*. Peter had written the following note for the play: 'First the story of sun and snow, then the story of the names, then the story of a child; now the dramatic poem: the whole thing will be called *Slow Homecoming*.' *The Lesson of Mont St-Victoire* sets up the story,

Children's Story relates the consequences. The four books make one whole, even though the story is told, and has to be told, in many different forms. *Slow Homecoming* is the bulkiest screenplay I've ever written. It begins in Alaska, and then moves to San Francisco, Denver, and then New York; the hero then flies to Austria and meets his siblings to discuss what should happen to the family house. I couldn't find any backers for it in Germany: neither the government subsidy bodies, nor television, nor a distribution company. Everyone was frightened of the project. Without German capital, it was impossible to get any backing from abroad. I had to give up, and directed *The Long Way Round* for the stage at the Salzburg Festival.

The failure of the film project left my production company in difficulties. I had Sam Shepard's *Transfiction* with me, and wrote a treatment in which the hero was really the manuscript. The film was to begin with a car smash in the desert. Two cars: in one a man on his own, in the other a couple. No witnesses. The man dies, and the couple, whose fault it was, decide to run off. The woman has a last look round the other car and finds a manuscript, which she takes with her. The couple are on their way across the United States; the woman reads the manuscript as they drive. It becomes more and more important to her: her dreams and imaginings are suddenly dominated by things that are in the manuscript.

I sent Sam the treatment. He was unimpressed and said he thought it was artificial and cerebral. But that didn't affect our desire to work together on something. He saw my films and I saw his plays; we told each other all kinds of stories and soon we had another idea. A man turns up, having crossed the Mexican border. He's lost his memory, he's as ignorant and helpless as a child. We developed the story from that point on. We had various ideas: to have his brother looking for him, to have him looking for his own past, looking for a woman ... We had to stop there; Sam had something else to get on with.

I started travelling. At first I imagined the film going all over America, from the Mexican border up to Alaska. Sam, though, thought we should stay in Texas: Texas was America in miniature. So I drove all over Texas. When I'd done that, I came round to his way to thinking.

In Salzburg I'd read the *Odyssey* for the first time. That myth couldn't have any viability in a European landscape, but it would go well in the western USA.

The town of Paris, Texas – on the banks of the Red River, up in the north near the state border with Oklahoma – suggested itself to us on account of its name. That amazing collision of Paris and Texas – the essences of Europe and America – straightaway crystallized many elements of the script: the name Paris, Texas, would symbolize the split within Travis. It was the place where his parents met and he was conceived. Mother and son suffered from the father's constant joke, 'I met my wife in Paris', and from his disappearance. Paris, Texas, became a place of separation. For Travis, it's a mythical place, where he has to reunite his own scattered family.

From the outset we thought of Travis's wife as being much younger than he was. Sam thought she should be a Texan. I knew that most of the cast would be American, and I really needed at least one European actress: she would be the link connecting Paris and Texas. I suggested Nastassia Kinski: Sam wouldn't have taken any other European actress.

I was delighted to be able to work with Robby Müller again, seven years after our last collaboration. We were determined to set about this film without any aesthetic models, no Walker Evans or Edward Hopper. More filmic, we said. It was to be our encounter with the landscape.

Tokyo-Ga

Tokyo-Ga came about quite spontaneously, a few months before *Paris, Texas*. The script for that was ready, the recce and other preparations complete; I was only waiting for Chris Sievernich to secure the backing. Then I was asked to go to Tokyo as part of a German film week there. The year before I'd made a short film in New York in diary form, commissioned by French television. Now I felt like having another stab at a documentary, commissioned or not.

I phoned Ed Lachman, who'd been my cameraman on *Nick's Film*. Him with his Aäton camera, and me with my Walkman into which I'd had a quartz built – we were a good team. Our initial intention was to film for a week, but we ended up staying for a fortnight. We weren't making a film about Tokyo, but trying to seek out Ozu's traces there. It took a while to get in touch with one of his lead actors, Ryu Chishu; until then we did some rather haphazard filming: leaving the hotel, in the *pachinko* rooms, in the underground, in the baseball stadia . . . Our only fixed points were our conversations with Ryu and with Ozu's cameraman, Yuharu Atsuta.

I saw the rushes for *Tokyo-Ga* only much later, after we'd finished filming *Paris, Texas*. I tried to edit both films at once, but it was too much. In the end, I edited *Tokyo-Ga* a full two years after shooting it. It made me realize that editing a documentary is a much more complicated business than editing a feature film. To find the logic of the images, and to provide them with a coherent form, all that's much harder than on a feature.

The editing took months; it got out of all proportion to the filming. I'd really lost touch with the images. It was as though they were someone else's. Besides, I'd concentrated on the sound while we were filming; I went around with headphones, and a microphone in my hand the whole time. As a result, I wasn't calling the shots, I was too preoccupied with the sound. That taught me a better understanding of sound engineers: sometimes, when they take off their cans, they're amazed to see what's going on around them. And I learned what an editor has to do too, how dispassionate he has to be. I felt great difficulty editing scenes I hadn't shot: I couldn't find my own subjective vision in them. It made me realize that on any subsequent diary film I make, I'll have to go behind the camera myself.

Until the End of the World

There's no other project I've pursued over such a long period as this one. I started writing in 1977, during my first visit to Australia. It was the continent that got me going. I'd come at it by an unusual route, not arriving in either of the great cities on the eastern seaboard, Sydney or Melbourne, but in Darwin, a very hot place in the far north of the country, near the tropics. From there I went into the interior and saw the red earth. I felt like making a film practically the moment I got there: it was a landscape that seemed to cry out for a science-fiction story. I was working on a story when a telegram came from San Francisco asking me to direct *Hammett*.

Seven years later, I revisited the same places, this time accompanied by

Solveig Dummartin. Nothing had changed: the scenery was still an incitement to fiction. A love story now joined my early drafts; there's a round-the-world trip before the arrival in Australia. (I've sort of seen the film I was envisaging ten years ago. It's *On the Beach* by Stanley Kramer, a very beautiful film, made in 1959 in Australia.) There are many languages spoken in my film: English, French, Russian, German, Chinese, Japanese, Spanish and Portuguese. Solveig will be in it. Rüdiger Vogler will be in it too. One inspiration for a film is wanting to have particular actors in it. In this case, there is another too: wanting to have particular images. Robby will shoot it in Cinemascope for the first time.

When I told the story to a friend, he said: 'Ah, I know what you're doing. You've always told the story of Odysseus running round the world and never managing to get home. Now you're telling the story of Penelope as she follows him.' The main character is a young woman, following a man she's fallen in love with, and who seems to be running away from her. The more she pursues him, the further he runs – only she's not sure why, given that the man is obviously afraid that it's not him she's after. He's on a mission and has to be alone. So he's afraid that she wants something else. Anyway, the woman pursues the man round the world, and she herself is pursued by a man who's still in love with her and unable to let her go.

The film was always going to be set in the year 2000. The tragi-comical thing about that is the fact that we're already in 1987, and there are barely twelve years to go. When I started planning it there were twenty-three. When I look at the old notes I made in 1977, I'm bewildered: where's the science fiction? All the technical innovations, the depiction of a futuristic lifestyle, all that seems almost banal, as though reality had caught up with my fantasy. It's amazing how quickly science fiction becomes obsolete. So you rewrite. If it goes on like that, the film won't be anything to do with science fiction, and I'll be lucky if I can get it made by 2000.

I worked on the script with Solveig for two years. We went round the world twice, doing the preparations for it. We took on an American scriptwriter, Michael Almereyda, and when we finally had the screenplay ready it was clear that it would take at least a year to make, and maybe more. The idea's become very expensive and involved. We envisaged shooting in fifteen countries, and even the preparations were like an Odyssey ... Again, it put my production company into difficulties. I wouldn't have been able to go on paying my staff if I hadn't taken on another film in the meantime.

Wings of Desire

In the last few years, since *Paris, Texas*, Berlin has been the place where I've stopped off. I started to feel at home there, in spite of the fact that I see the city with the eyes of someone who's spent a lot of time away.

Up until now, the stories in my films were always told from the point of view of a main character. This time, I rejected the idea of some returning hero who rediscovers Berlin and Germany for himself. I couldn't imagine the character through whose eyes I would see Berlin; such a person could only have been another version of myself. Besides, Travis had been a man returning to a city.

I really don't know what gave me the idea of angels. One day I wrote 'Angels' in my notebook, and the next day 'The unemployed'. Maybe it was because I was reading Rilke at the time – nothing to do with films – and realizing as I read how much of his writing is inhabited by angels. Reading Rilke every night, perhaps I got used to the idea of angels being around.

After a while I began to doubt whether it would amount to a film. I tried to push the idea away, but it was never quite extinguished.

I filled a whole notebook, but it still didn't add up to a film. Usually, a line soon emerges that enables you to fix on the characters and their relationships. But with angels you could do anything, there were connections all over the place, you could go anywhere. You could cross the Wall, pass through windows into people's houses, and anyone, a passer-by, passengers in the underground, was suddenly the hero of a potential film. It was scary: there was too much freedom for the imagination. Even more so because there were going to be several angels. Berlin is still governed by the Four Powers, so I thought you might have four angels: American, British, French and Russian. But that made it too schematic. Then for a time, the angels were ex-airmen, a kind of aviators' club, like in Howard Hawks's *Only Angels Have Wings*. By and by, we boiled it down to keep just what mattered: what the angels see. The story's told from the angels' point of view – but how do you show what angels see?

There was also another, completely different, starting-point for *Wings of Desire*. At the end of *Paris, Texas* there's a scene between Nastassia and little Hunter in the hotel: he goes to his mother, she takes him in her arms. There was something liberating about that scene for me: it was a feeling I was sure would have repercussions on my next film, whatever it was. (The last scene, when Travis walks away: I let him go the way I do, and all my previous male characters left with him. They now live in an old people's home on the edge of Paris, Texas.) So I badly wanted to have a woman as the main character. For a long time I wondered about making one of the angels female. But I wanted this angel to become human, and I thought it was more interesting to have the human being a woman and the angel a man who accepts mortality for her sake.

I wanted to start filming in the autumn, but there was no screenplay ready. I always feel a kind of block about writing anything that's meant to turn into a scene. I tell myself that if I write it, it'll be ruined as a scene, because there'll be nothing left to invent.

The angels had to speak poetically, so language became especially important. Having made four films in English, I badly wanted to return to my mother tongue and I wanted the dialogues to be particularly beautiful. I called my archangel Peter Handke. He had just finished a novel and said: 'I'm completely drained. I don't have any words left in me, everything I had is in the novel.' But then he added: 'Maybe if you come down here and tell me your story, then I can help you out with a few scenes. But no more; nothing structural, no screenplay.' I drove down to Salzburg to see him and told him all I knew about my angels. We spent a week thinking up a dozen key situations in a possible plot, and Peter started writing on the basis of that.

Every week, all through September, I would get an envelope full of dialogue, without any direction or description, like in a stage play. There was no contact between us; he wrote, and I prepared the film. There was a growing gulf between the work Peter was doing in Salzburg and the film that was gradually taking shape in Berlin, in discussions with the actors, and the physical preparations. Peter's scenes – though beautiful and poetic – were like monoliths from heaven. But they didn't fit: there was a complete discord between his dialogues, the scenes we envisaged and the locations we'd decided on.

Preparations for the production were not yet complete and the sets not yet ready. The angels had no costumes, no make-up, nothing. We began filming, beginning with the children right at the start. I was absolutely convinced that if we went on preparing, we'd lose everything. Yes, we'll know exactly what we're doing, but it'll mean we'll make a worked-out film. On the other hand, being in a state of confusion will force us to find something for the angels.

The idea for the film had suggested itself to me in black and white; Berlin needed that, and so did the angels: they were unable to touch things, they didn't know the physical world, and so it was logical that they had no colours either. Also, black and white is associated with the world of dreams. It was exciting to imagine the world of the angels in black and white, with colour appearing at odd moments in the film, as a new experience. I knew that Henri Alekan, who didn't know Berlin, would reveal a new and unfamiliar view of it: he has the ability to create incorporeal shapes with light, as though he himself had access to this faerie universe through the mystery of light. At the beginning, Henri wanted the angels to be transparent. It was difficult to persuade him that it would make it impossible to tell the story from that premise. His idea of transparency has survived in two shots, where the angel Damiel 'steals' objects, first a stone, then a pencil: the objects don't actually move, they stay put on the table; Damiel just takes their essence.

The names for the angels came out of a dictionary of angels: Damiel and Cassiel. As I was devising the film, filling up notebooks, I never asked myself about the casting: photographs of Solveig, Bruno Ganz and Otto Sander hung on my wall and inspired me from the beginning.

As in *Until the End of the World*, Solveig was part of the film from the start; it was clear she would be in it. She had done tightrope work at a circus school in Paris, but as an amateur. A circus is a privileged spot because of the presence of children, and with all the waste ground in Berlin there is always a circus there: that suggested to me that the woman be a trapeze artiste. Besides, I wanted her work to be dangerous – so that she would charm Damiel, who was never himself in any danger of falling. And so I imagined the girl as a trapeze artiste, flying under the big top with tinsel wings. When the angel saw her, he would laugh, no question. And perhaps fall in love . . .

When I told Solveig about it, she wasn't sure if I meant it. But the next day she went back to her trapeze course with Pierre Bergam in Paris. She dismissed the idea of having a double: she wanted to perform the trapeze number herself, like a professional. A few weeks later, I started on the preparations in Berlin; I found a circus and an old trainer, a Hungarian, who'd formerly been a *porteur*. He'd done work on a Shakespeare comedy with Bruno and Otto at the Schaubühne, and had taught Otto tightrope-walking. He was called Kovacs, like all Hungarians. Every day he worked with Solveig in a real circus, five hours a day. And he said to me: 'She's got talent. Give me six weeks, and she'll do the part.' He succeeded in making a trapeze artiste out of her. One day she fell from a height of five metres, on to her back, and Kovacs straightaway sent her up again. She went on with her number in a state of concussion. Two days later, we filmed her trapeze routine.

The parts of Curt Bois and Peter Falk weren't added till much later, when the filming was already under way. Bruno and Otto introduced me to Curt Bois. (In 1983 they had made a documentary with him and Bernhard Minetti called *Memory*.) In a very early version of the story that I told Peter Handke, there was the character of an old archangel who lives in a library. Peter had no use for him, but on the wall in front of his writing desk was a reproduction of Rembrandt's *Homer*: an old man seated and talking – to whom? Originally Rembrandt had him speaking to a disciple, but the picture had been cut in two and the storyteller had been separated from his listener, so he's now merely soliloquizing. Peter was very fond of the painting and changed my idea of the archangel to an immortal poet. Now I, for my part, had no idea of how to integrate Homer into my script. Finally we had Homer living in a library, and Peter's dialogues became a voice inside his head. Curt Bois was neither man nor angel, but both at once, because he's as old as the cinema itself.

The last person to join the angelic ranks was Peter Falk. His part was a sort of comedy idea: he had to be some extremely famous figure, and you would gradually realize he was a former angel. At first I thought of painters, writers and so on, even politicians, someone like Willy Brandt, but you couldn't film with those people. And he had to be someone so famous that he'd be instantly recognized, and you'd say to yourself: Ah, so he's an angel too . . . In the end I got around to thinking of actors, and then, by necessity, of American actors. They are the only world-famous actors. One evening I got Peter Falk on the telephone and told him this bewildering story of guardian angels, circuses, a trapeze artiste and an American actor who charms his former colleagues. There was a pause, and then he asked me if I could send him a script. I said: 'No, I can't. There's nothing in writing about this ex-angel. I can't even send you a single page: he's just an idea.' He liked that; if I'd sent him a script he might not have accepted. But since there was nothing to go on at all, he said: 'Ah, I've worked like that before with Cassavetes, and honestly I prefer working without a script.'

We spoke only twice on the telephone. He landed in Berlin one Friday night, we talked about his scenes over the weekend, and filmed them the following week. He so liked the crew and the work that he ended up staying another week. He kept hoping we might film some more scenes with him. Since he didn't know Berlin at all, he was for ever going for walks. It was a bit like his part in the film: we kept looking for him and he was always off walking somewhere.

October 1987